Conan spun to [...] second korga. [...] clawed at him [...] loud *click!* but [...] and swung his [...] but the angle was bad and the sharpened iron merely tore a fist-sized chunk out of the beast's side. The monster howled liquidly and backed away a pace, lashing its thick tail in rage.

Conan sensed the approach of the third attacker, but he could not better its speed. The thing barreled into him, knocking him from his feet. Falling, Conan lost his grip on his sword, and it clattered to the ground half a body-length away.

Catlike, the Cimmerian twisted, turning his fall into a dive. He rolled and recovered, but the third korga charged him before he could retrieve his blade. The pointed teeth loomed large in the gaping maw, and Conan drew back his fist. He would ram his hand down his throat. Maybe he could choke it before it bit his arm off—

The monster screeched and stumbled, then fell forward to land face down at the Cimmerian's feet. What—?

The woman's spear stood embedded in the beast's back. She had sacrificed her weapon to save him!

CONAN

THE FREE LANCE

The Adventures of Conan
published by Tor Books

CONAN

THE FREE LANCE
BY
STEVE PERRY

TOR

A TOM DOHERTY ASSOCIATES BOOK
NEW YORK

CONAN THE FREE LANCE

Copyright © 1990 by Conan Properties, Inc.

A TOR Book
Published by Tom Doherty Associates, Inc.
49 West 24 Street
New York, N.Y. 10010

Cover art by Kirk Reinert

ISBN: 0-812-50690-1   Can. ISBN: 0-812-50691-X

Library of Congress Catalog Card Number:

First edition: February 1990

Printed in the United States of America

0 9 8 7 6 5 4 3 2 1

This book is for Dianne; and for Ray Capella, who is better at this than I.

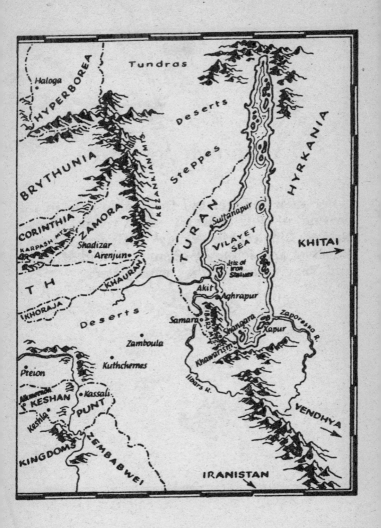

Acknowledgments

For their indirect but invaluable help in the writing of this book, I must thank George Reeves, Clayton Moore, Jock Mahoney, Duncan Renaldo, and Johnny Weissmuller. And Modesty and Travis, though they came later.

PROLOGUE

Ten million years before the birth of the first man, the tallest peak in what would be called in dimly future times the Karpash Mountains stood in ice-capped majesty near what was to become the border between Corinthia and Zamora. It had no name then, there being no creatures with language to make names; later, it would be called Mount Turio. On a cold winter's day and without warning, an explosion shook the earth to its roots, and the top half of the mountain blew off. Pulverized rock formed ebon and stormy clouds that hid the face of the sun; glowing lava spewed and flowed down, feeding upon and consuming giant trees flattened for two days' march in any direction from the wounded mountain. The sweeping hand of destruction wiped away a hundred thousand animals, scouring the land with a stone wind that spared no living thing exposed to its abrasive touch.

Halfway to the edge of the world, beasts paused in their paths at the sound of the mountain vomiting itself up and darkening the skies.

It was a noise to rival the scream of a god.

After a million years, the crater left by the titanic explosion became a lake as large as a small sea.

After ten million years, the scars of the cataclysm had mostly been erased by time and weather, smoothed by winds and rain and snow and sun. The great crater lake remained, however, icy and clear and deep.

In the center of that vast lake, nameless and mostly unknown to the eyes and thoughts of men, the floating mat of a unique plant thrived upon the surface of the azure water. The growth was called Sargasso weed by those with a need for such names. Dense the weed was, and buoyant and thick enough to support the weight of a low, rambling structure large enough to house a thousand men. A careful man could walk from the center of the Palace of the Sargasso for most of a day and not reach the closest edge of the living island, though finding water was seldom a problem. In places the mat was carefully thinned by predators who lived below and sought to trap prey; a misstep would send the unwary to a watery death in the jaws of some hungry denizen spawned in the lake's cold, dark depths. Even should a man avoid the quicksandlike traps in the Sargasso, he was ever at risk, for things also lived in the tangled growth above the chilly water, things that had over centuries developed a taste for human flesh.

In the center of this construction of nature and man, in the bowels of the sprawling and low castle, dwelled the one known as the Abet Blasa, Dimma of the Fogs, called by some the Mist Mage.

Although the roof of the chamber bore several large openings covered with sheets of clearest quartz to allow a goodly measure of the sun's light to flow into the room, a perpetual fog enshrouded Dimma where he sat upon a throne of carved woods and ivory. Indeed, Dimma's form itself seemed to blend with the swirling mist. He had no hard edges, appearing as insubstantial as the grayness he wore about himself as a billowing cloak.

Into the shifting grayness came a thing that upon land could pass for a man. Once the ancestors of this creature had dwelled Below, but through the arcane arts of the Mist Mage, these beasts had been elevated, both in form and in intelligence. Dimma called them selkies, and through his crafting, had made them into most useful servants. No longer were they simple beasts, and although they could pretend to be human upon the land, in the water they reverted magically into something from a man's nightmare.

The selkie's name was Kleg, and it spoke in a

singsong tone, more as if using some stringed instrument than a true voice. "My lord, I am here."

The wavering image of the Mist Mage turned toward the selkie. Dimma focused his attention upon the creature to whom he was literally a god. "Speak to me of your mission, Kleg."

"My lord. Six days' ride from here upon the back of the packbeast you created stands the Tree Folk's forest. We have determined that the . . . ingredients you seek can be found therein."

The Mist Mage leaned forward. His face shimmered as a wisp of fog passed over—and through—it, becoming for a moment more sharply etched. Kleg felt a spasm of fear clutch at his bowels, turning them cold.

"And have you brought these ingredients to me?"

"No, my lord. The Tree Folk are powerful and vigilant. In the attempt to secure that which you seek, four of your servants were destroyed. Only two of us remained, and our escape was a near thing."

Dimma leaned back in his throne, the wood and ivory visible to the selkie through his master's body. "You are as powerful as three men, Kleg."

"Even so, my lord. The Tree Folk themselves are agile and strong, and they control their grove so that even such as we could not overcome them."

The Abet Blasa sat silently for a moment.

"You are certain that which I require can be obtained from the Tree Folk?"

"Certain, my lord."

"Then it does not matter how agile or strong they are. I will have what I must have. You must do whatever is necessary to accomplish this task. Go and gather your brothers. A dozen, a hundred, as many as you think needed. All the beasts of the Sargasso are at your disposal."

"Your word is my life," Kleg said as he bowed and backed from the chamber.

Indeed, Dimma thought as he watched the selkie leave. Your life and the lives of ten times ten thousand are nothing compared to what I must have.

Dimma rose and floated across the huge room. Where he moved, the fog thickened about him, centering upon his person as if flowing from his body outward, and indeed that was the case.

Five hundred years past, Dimma had been a young and foolish student of the arts. In his travels, he had grown arrogant in his power. One fateful day, he sought to test the mettle of the Wizard of Koth, a shriveled and toothless old man whose reputation Dimma had carelessly deemed larger than his true power.

Dimma had been wrong. Toothless he might be, but the Wizard of Koth was not without a fierce and sorcerous bite. In the ensuing battle, the old man had died, but not without first laying his curse upon the cocky Dimma.

As he lay breathing his last, the old man had managed a smile. "You are a hard one," he'd said. "Flint and fired iron, and giving away nothing. But from this day forth, it shall not be so. You shall give away all; your body will become that of a man of mist, and ever shall you dwell in fog. So shall it be said, so shall it be done."

The old man had died then, and Dimma had been unworried. A dying curse was to be expected; he had weathered more than a few as he had slain various adepts. They meant nothing. He, Dimma, had stalked wizards of the Ring and of the Square. He had bested the yellow Seers of Turan, crushed the dark-skinned spell singers of Zembabwei. One more mage meant little to him.

At first.

A month after his duel with the Wizard of Koth, Dimma sought his pleasure with a woman. He reached for her, and—

His hand passed through her body!

Dimma fled from the encounter and convinced himself he had fallen prey to an illusion, a trick resulting from much wine and too little light, and at first, it seemed to be so. But during the ensuing months, the old Kothian's curse had flowered into a bitter, airy blossom. Dimma became more and more insubstantial, and there seemed no cure for it. It came and it went without reason.

He was not without skill, and he utilized all of it to rid himself of the geas, but it was to little avail. More and more of his time was spent as a creature less of flesh than of vapor. Days, sometimes weeks would pass before he regained the flesh. He could still perform most of his own conjurations, using one of his servants as a stand-in for those things needing a physical hand, but the other pleasures of the body were lost to him. He could not eat or drink or enjoy erotic pleasures with women, nor could he feel the sensations of heat or cold or texture. He became a kind of ghost, living in perpetual fog, a thing more brother to mist than to man.

Five hundred years is a long time, however, and the constant searching eventually turned up clues to a cure for the affliction. From a sacred cave in Stygia came a tattered scroll with part of the cure; from a ruined temple on Siptah's Isle came another part. Dimma's agents roamed to the Black Kingdoms—Kush, Darfar, Keshan, and Punt—as well as to the northern cold lands of Vanaheim and Asgard. No place was too distant to reach if some hope might be offered for a cure, no cost too great. Some of the spells collected stretched from before the time Atlantis had been swallowed by the sea.

At last, Dimma had the pieces of the puzzle he needed, all save one. And the final item lay practically in his own realm! He would have it at any cost. It had been twenty years since last he managed a few moments of solidity; he never knew for what reason or when he might be given a brief respite from his curse. Now he saw the end of his torment looming only days or weeks away, and he would use every bit of his not inconsiderable power to achieve that end, no matter if it required destruction of a kingdom!

Dimma felt a stray breeze lift and shift him sideways. Someone had left a door ajar or a window open, and that someone would die for the error. Soon he would not have to suffer such indignities, and woe to any man or anything that stood in Dimma's way.

Woe, indeed.

ONE

The narrow mountain path lay upon a steep grade, patches of loose gravel strewn over it, but the young man walking the route did so with both agility and grace. He was, after all, a Cimmerian, and those from the mountains of his birth learned to climb as soon as they could walk. The man was called Conan, and the slanting rays of the setting sun reflected from smoldering blue eyes framed by a thick, black square-cut mane that touched wide, heavy shoulders. Conan wore the hastily tanned hide of a wolf over his brawny back, short leathern breeches, and sandals with thongs that laced up around his muscular calves. The chilly mountain air nipped at the places where his skin lay bare, but he ignored the cold stoically. After the confinement of the vast underground system of the Black Cave in which he and his

then companions almost died a dozen times,
the open air was welcome, no matter what its
temperature.

He was bound for Zamora, for the wicked
city of Shadizar, wherein he intended to ply
what he hoped would be the lucrative trade of
thief. It was said that a quick wit, a strong
arm, and a sharp blade were all a man needed
to survive in Shadizar. Add to that a light
touch and quick feet, and genuine prosperity
could supposedly be had. Conan meant to find
out if this was true. He was young, but his
short life had given him a wealth of experience
and he stood ready to add material wealth to
his experience.

The trip thus far had taken much longer than
he had thought it would; the gods kept putting
obstacles in his path, albeit that some of them
were attractive women, and his adventures had
been more than a little perilous. Necromancers
and wizards and monsters had bedeviled
Conan—like most honest men, he had no use
for magic—and between the beautiful desert
woman Elashi, the long-dead zombie woman
Tuanne, and the evil witch mistress of the
caves, Chuntha, his desire for women of late
had been more than slaked. He was alone
again, and happy for it.

The path took a sharp turning to the right a
few steps below where Conan walked, and from
around that turn came a noise.

It was small, the sound barely enough for the
Cimmerian's sharp ears to discern, but he

stopped his progress immediately and drew the ancient blued-iron sword ensheathed at his side. The blade was solid and heavy, the hilt unadorned leather wrapping over the metal tang, and it had cost Conan a bout with a long-dead warrior who had been reduced to a living skeleton. The blade was of razor sharpness, kept so by Conan's application of whetstones after even the smallest usage.

Gripping the sword in two hands, after the manner of the warrior priests he had met in a mountain temple, Conan moved along the path, taking great care to avoid dislodging any of the small stones littering the hard ground. The sound could mean nothing, a rock contracting in the cold or a small animal scurrying about chasing an insect, but Conan had not survived this long in a dangerous world by taking foolish chances. Crom was his god, and Crom gave a man a measure of strength and wit at birth, then left the rest up to him. Any of Crom's children who failed to use both gifts properly need not waste breath trying to call for the god's help.

Keeping close to the wall of rock that bounded the path on the right, Conan reached the edge of the turn. Raising the sword so that it would not betray his presence, he quickly stepped around the corner and brought the blade down again, pointed at throat level.

Just ahead the path widened considerably where the mountain had been worn away by time and weather, and in the deep cleft of rock stood a half-naked woman with a long spear, her back to the stone, half-encircled by five man-sized dragons. A sixth dragon lay on its back nearby in a large pool of what Conan supposed was its own ichor. Clutched in its claws was a scrap of cloth that seemed to match the breechclout that was now the spearwoman's sole garment.

The cloth had been a costly trophy for the giant lizard, so it would seem.

Conan's recent adventures were much in his mind, so much so that his first thought upon viewing the scene in front of him was: Oh, no. Another *woman*.

The greenish-gray-scaled dragons stood upright, had long tails, pointed snouts and yellow eyes, and were not without peripheral vision. The nearest one either saw or smelled or heard the Cimmerian and flicked a glance in the man's direction. So still was Conan that the thing looked back toward its female prey, then snapped its attention to Conan a second time. It made a burbling hiss, drawing the gazes of the other dragons.

Conan wondered how fast they were. Could he turn and flee without being caught? Well, likely not, the path being rather steep around the turn, and besides, there was the woman. Now that he looked closer, he could see bloody gouges on one of her shoulders, doubtless put there by the thing that had stolen her garment, and despite his danger, Conan had time to notice that the shoulder was well rounded and firm, and the breast next to it also well rounded and firm. Indeed, the woman's torso was more muscular than most women's he had seen, sinews shifting under the tanned skin as she shifted the spear in her grasp. It was not unattractive, the sight, and despite his resolve to avoid women for a time, he felt himself curious about this one.

The first dragon hissed and burbled again, and two of the other dragons shifted toward Conan, leaving two to watch the woman.

"Best you run, stranger," the woman said, her voice quite calm. "These are Korga, the Pili's hunting dogs."

Conan did not know who the Pili were, nor did he care. To the woman he said, "I am going south. Are these . . . ah, Korga apt to allow me to pass?"

"Nay, stranger."

"Well, then, I know how to deal with dogs, no matter what their shape," Conan said, loosening his grip on the sword, then re-forming it. To the dragons, he said, "Here, curs!"

But he did not wait for the Korga to gather themselves. Raising the heavy sword over his right shoulder as a man raises an ax for splitting firewood, he sprang. The closest dragon seemed startled by the man's sudden charge. It flashed wicked teeth, pointed and as long as a man's little finger, but before it could do more than bare these deadly fangs, Conan was upon it. The blade whistled in the cool evening air, and when it landed, it was not wood that split

but the beast's skull. Gore splashed and the
thing dropped, dead before it sprawled on the
rocky ground.

Conan spun to his left to meet the charge of
the second Korga. The thing hissed and burbled and clawed at the man, and its jaws
snapped shut with a loud click, but missed as
Conan dodged backward and swung the sword.
The blade met scaled flesh, but the angle was
bad and the sharpened iron merely tore a
fist-size chunk of the beast's side away and
flung it from the mountain. The monster howled
liquidly and backed away a pace, lashing its
thick tale in rage.

Conan sensed the approach of the third attacker, but it moved faster than he'd thought
possible, and quick as the Cimmerian was, he
could not better the dragon's speed. The thing
barreled into him, knocking him from his feet.
In the fall, Conan lost his grip on his sword,
and it clattered to the ground half a body
length away.

Catlike, the Cimmerian twisted, turning his
fall into a dive. He rolled and came up, but the
third Korga charged him before he could retrieve his blade. The pointed teeth loomed
large in the gaping maw, and Conan drew back
his fist. He would ram his hand down its
throat. Maybe he could choke it before it bit
his arm off—

The dragon screeched and stumbled, then fell
forward to land facedown at the Cimmerian's
feet. What . . . ?

The woman's spear stood embedded deeply in the beast's back. She had sacrificed her weapon to save him!

Conan dived again, snatched up his blade, and sprinted toward the woman. She had fetched up a rock the size of a hen's egg, and as Conan ran, he saw her throw the stone at the nearer of the two Korga watching her. The missile struck the thing squarely on the chest, knocking it backward. The creature clasped its front claws to the injury, hissing and howling as might a cat tossed into a fire.

The Korga Conan had wounded earlier sought to stop the man's charge, but Conan's powerful right arm and shoulder arced the sword in a one-handed cut that ripped out the beast's throat. It fell, mortally wounded.

Three down, two more to go.

The woman bent for another rock, but the second of the two Korga she faced hopped in and grabbed her. It lifted her clear off the ground, and Conan realized he would arrive too late to save her; it opened its mouth to bite off her head—

She poked the monster in the eye with her finger.

The Korga dropped the woman and clapped its claws to its injured eye; it danced around in a circle with the pain and outrage. Unfortunately for the Korga, that was to be its last dance, for Conan held his sword point forward and ran the monster through, spitting it neatly. If a lizard the size of a man could look surprised, this one did as it fell, its spirit already on the way to the Gray Lands to join those of its dead brothers.

The last Korga found itself with a bruised chest and all alone against two opponents. The woman came up with another rock and hurled it with good effect, smacking into the Korga's belly as Conan stalked forward with his bloody weapon lifted. The Korga apparently decided it had had enough, for it turned and left in a great hurry. The woman tossed another rock after it, but missed, and the thing fled down the mountain path much faster than a running man could hope to match.

Not that Conan was really interested in chasing it. He took a few halfhearted steps after the thing, waving his sword and yelling, but the farther away it got, the better, as far as he was concerned.

When he turned back toward the woman, she was retrieving her garment from the claws of the dead Korga. Conan watched as she donned the ripped but still serviceable sleeveless jerkin and pulled it shut with a thin belt. A pity, that, Conan thought, because she was quite a well-endowed woman, for all her muscle. Those feelings toward women he had thought slaked now reared again, as if the past months had not existed.

"I owe you my life, stranger," she said, and smiled.

Conan gestured with his sword at the spear

standing from the killed beast. "And I owe you mine. Consider us even on that score."

"Done. I am Cheen, medicine woman of the Tree Folk." She went to retrieve her spear.

"I am called Conan, of Cimmeria."

"Well met, Conan, from the top of the world."

"You know Cimmeria?"

"We have heard of it. My grove is but half a day's journey from here. Would you stop and rest and eat with us?"

Conan had been several weeks on the trail and in no hurry for much company, but this woman who could slay dragons with such offhand calmness intrigued him. "Aye, I suppose my journey would not suffer greatly for such hospitality."

"Come, then. It will be dark soon and best we find a safe place for camp. Night travel in the mountains is not without its dangers."

Conan looked at the dead beasts. "Nor would daylight seem to be altogether trouble free."

"There are things in these hills after dark that make the Pili's dogs look like tame pups," she said.

"By all means, then, let us find a campsite."

As they moved along the mountain path, Cheen told Conan of the Pili.

"They are like men," she said, "but also distant kin to the Korga. Warm blood flows in their veins, but it is lizard blood to be sure. They inhabit the desert two days' journey past my grove. They eat people when they capture them."

Conan considered this. "Can one travel south to Shadizar without traversing this Pili desert?"

"There are ways to skirt their territory, yes."

"Good." Conan was afraid of no man in a stand-up fight, but the idea of walking across a wasteland of maneaters who used tame dragons for dogs held little appeal.

None, actually.

He did not ask what Cheen had been doing alone in such dangerous territory, it being none of his business, but she volunteered the information. "I have been for the last moon seeking a plant that grows in these hills. A kind of toadstool used in our religious ceremonies. Such fungi grow only on the dung of the wild mountain goats, these goats unfortunately being also a favorite prey of the Pili when they cannot obtain human meat."

Conan grunted noncommittally. Religion was another form of magic; he preferred to have no truck with it either, but he did not begrudge those who did.

"I have found enough for our next True Seeing." Hereupon she opened a small purse tied to her belt and showed Conan some dank-smelling little brown mushrooms. "Properly mixed and consecrated, the brew made from these allows one to see one's god."

Again Conan shrugged. He could do without such sights. He had more in mind filling his senses with good wine, better food, well-made weapons, and well-made women, all of which would be available to a rich thief in Shadizar. Let the priests see to the gods, a man had enough to worry about without that.

As the sun touched the western horizon, they came upon a wide ledge twice a tall man's height above the trail and climbed up to it. Cheen climbed well, better in fact than Conan had ever seen any woman climb. She was like a spider as she moved up the rock, finding toe and fingerholds he would have thought impossible for any save a Cimmerian.

Once on the ledge, they built tall cairns of loose rock on both ends so that nothing larger than a rabbit could approach without tumbling the barriers. A dead bush on the rock face gave them tinder and fuel for a small fire, and it was but the work of a moment for Conan to strike sparks from a flint and a hardened chunk of melted iron he carried for that purpose to start the fire. He had a skin of water and several strips of dried squirrel jerky the two of them shared as night laid its dark shroud over the land.

The night was cold and the fire offered but a small warmth. Conan was of a mind to offer to share his wolf-pelt cloak with Cheen. He did so, but she only smiled and told him it was not necessary.

Perhaps, he thought, it was because he had more in mind to share with her than merely the cloak and she somehow sensed this. Women were adept at knowing such things, he had found, though the how of it had eluded him. In his travels, Conan had met many men, but never one who claimed to understand the minds of women. Well, no, there had been one who said he knew *exactly* what women wanted, but he had also thought that the world was round, like a ball, and that he could fly by flapping his arms like a bird. That one had tried his second theory from the roof of the tallest structure in the village in which he had lived, a water tower ten times a man's height. He had not survived the test. Mad as a pig full of wine, he had been.

He wondered at times if a man who truly understood women existed anywhere.

With those thoughts in his mind, Conan drifted into a sound slumber.

TWO

The morning broke crisply, the sun's rays slanting over the eastern hilltops to paint pink and yellow the ledge upon which Conan and Cheen lay. Conan stirred easily from sleep, alert and a bit stiff from his bed on solid rock.

The woman awakened as Conan rekindled the fire and began to warm his hands against the morning's chill.

"Slept you well?" she asked.

"Aye. As always."

After sharing the last of Conan's dried meat and rinsing it down with water from his skin, they descended the cliff face. Once again, Conan was impressed by the woman's agility. She moved like the snow monkeys of Cimmeria, never a slip or slide as she clambered downward.

Conan, never loath to recognize a notable skill, remarked upon Cheen's ability as they attained the trail.

She smiled. "We do some climbing where I come from. But I confess that I am least among those who have real talent at it. It is good that I am a medicine woman, for I would make a poor hunter."

Conan did not speak to this, but he was surprised. If she were the least climber among her people, what must the best be like? Perhaps they could even rival Cimmerians for agility.

As the sun rose to his highest perch, Conan followed Cheen downward toward a green valley in the distance. Aye, it was as if some god had a particular fondness for the hue, splashing verdaccio and emerald and olive everywhere.

The path twisted and turned upon itself as it worked its serpentine way around the mountain's side. Because of the circuitous nature of the hike, Conan did not see the forest until it practically stared them in the face. For a moment, he wondered if perhaps his hearing had gone bad, for to be so close to such a large wood, surely there should have been sounds his ears could detect?

But, no. The Cimmerian's eyes gave him the truth after a moment. The forest was in fact much farther away than first he had thought. The trees were of such proportions that they appeared like a glen of normal oaks, but Conan quickly realized that these trees were much larger than any he had seen before. There were hundreds of them, and unless Conan was very much mistaken, this grove of trees was full of giants, thrice the height of the tallest he had ever seen before. Crom, they must be fifty times the height of a man or more, massive plants that reached for the roof of the world.

As the pair drew nearer the grove of giants, Conan saw that there were houses built in the branches, an entire village mounted in the sky. Some of the constructions were relatively low to the ground, not more than ten spans up; some were much higher. There was no undergrowth, the ground being bare save for a carpet of dead leaves. He wondered whether this was because the thick canopy stopped light and rain from reaching the ground or if it were from design.

Had Conan half a dozen brothers his own size, it would have been impossible for them to link hands and surround the largest of the wooden monsters; even the smaller trees dwarfed the biggest normal trunk Conan had ever beheld.

"My grove," Cheen said.

"Your people live in the trees," Conan said.

"Aye. We are born, we live, and we die there."

"I can see how it is you know something of climbing."

"For a groundling, you have no small ability yourself." She smiled at him. "Especially seeing how ... large you are. None of our men approach your size."

They reached the base of the nearest tree. Conan looked up into the crown. The mighty

limbs extended from the trunk in a rough
circle, narrowing as they went up. The bark
was smooth to his touch, a reddish color with
patches peeled away to show a lighter color
underneath. The leaves were long, triple-pointed,
and the size of a man's hand, a dark, waxy
green that was almost black in color.

There at the bottom of the tree was a skin
the size of a shield stretched tightly over what
seemed a hollow. Cheen used the butt end of
her spear to rap the skin, which boomed like a
drum. She tapped on the tree drum for a time,
a rhythmic musical pattern. A few moments
after she finished her drumming, something
dropped from the lower branches toward them.

Instantly Conan drew his sword and made
ready to cut the falling mass.

"Hold," Cheen said. "There is no danger."

Indeed Conan saw this even as she spoke.
What fell from above was a kind of ladder.
Conan moved closer to examine it and saw that
it was plaited from strands of flexible vine, a
thick rope with hollow knots that formed foot
and handholds. He sheathed his blade.

"What if some attacker came and pounded
up your drum?"

"Each of the Tree Folk has his or her own
song," she said. "No two are alike. The watch
knows them all. A strange song would likely
draw a spear or shower of arrows."

Conan nodded. Attacking those who lived in
the trees would be a difficult task. A dozen men
with axes might labor a day to chop down a

single tree, and a rain of arrows, spears, or even rocks would make such a chore dangerous and unpleasant at best. The lack of under-growth would keep a fire from being a threat to those above, and it would take a large fire indeed to light one of the trunks. Conan took all this in with a practiced, albeit young mili-tary eye. He would not wish to lead the army of men who would make war on these Tree Folk.

"Shall we go up?" Cheen asked.

"After you," Conan said.

His courtesy was rewarded when he looked up as Cheen climbed a span above him. Her legs were not unpleasant to look upon.

As they left the vine rope, a short, stout woman greeted Cheen. This was the watch, and she was armed with a spear and an obsidian dagger as long as Conan's forearm. A bow and a quiverful of arrows leaned against the main trunk nearby, and a pile of rocks each as big as a man's head was held in place by vines next to the bow. As Conan had surmised earlier, coming up uninvited might be a perilous adventure.

Even a normal man would have little trouble balancing upon the thick branch upon which Conan followed Cheen. It was as wide as Conan's shoulders and the smooth bark had been shaved so that it was flat under his bare feet. He had removed his sandals and hung them over one shoulder for the climb and he saw no need to replace them.

Ahead loomed a large structure. This had been built from a platform on the branch upon which Conan now trod, and the edifice extended upward to connect to several other limbs. Conan noticed that the house was structured of the same wood that formed the giant tree, various-sized branches lashed together with vines like the one they'd ascended on. It was obviously of human construction, but looked like nothing so much as a giant wasp nest or beehive. Standing at the doorway to the building were two women dressed similarly to Cheen. Each woman was as well thewed as the medicine woman, and each held a short spear that rested its butt upon the wooden platform that formed a stoop to the house.

More women. Where were the men?

The guards nodded at Cheen, and she entered the house. Conan followed her. Holes in the roof provided sufficient light so that the Cimmerian could see. The room bore a long, low pallet against one wall and a carved chair in the center that faced a window opposite the door. Seated in the chair was an old woman, hair like snow, face eroded by time and sun. She wore a multihued green cloak wrapped about her body, the bright dyes almost luminous in the dim light. Her arms were bare, and though she was old, the lines of her arms and shoulders were deeply etched with tight muscle.

"Ho, Vares!" Cheen called.

The old woman turned away from her window and smiled at Cheen. "Ho, Cheen! It went well, your quest?"

Cheen lifted the bag containing the mushrooms she had shown Conan. "Yes, mistress. We can call the gods once again."

Vares nodded. "This is good. I had thought the next time I saw them might be after crossing the Gray Lands." She looked pointedly at Conan. "You have brought us a guest?"

"Aye, mistress. This is Conan of Cimmeria. When I was beset by the Pili's dogs at Donar Pass, he came to my aid."

The old woman smiled. "Accept my gratitude, Conan of Cimmeria. I should have hated to lose my eldest daughter."

"It was a mutual effort," Conan said.

Vares laughed. "What is this? A man who does not brag?"

Conan looked at Cheen, one eyebrow raised in question.

Cheen said, "Among our people, the men are great ... storytellers. Sometimes they embroider their tales with, ah, exaggerations."

"I have seen no men here," Conan said. This was perhaps blunt, but in Cimmeria, no one was faulted for directness. In some of the more so-called civilized lands through which he had traveled, it seemed that lying was a virtue, a thing that Conan could not understand.

"Ah. Come and look, then," Vares said. "Tair is teaching Hok the spring dance." She pointed toward the uncovered window.

Conan moved to look.

Leading away from Vares's house was a branch that thinned considerably after only a short distance. The limbs of the next tree intertwined with those of the one in which Conan stood, passing above and below; indeed, there was within his sight a virtual forest of arm- and leg-thick branches, mostly bare of leaves.

Running at speed along one of the branches was a short, well-made man dressed only in a sea green breechcloth. He ran as if the branch were as wide as a town road, and he laughed as he moved. Behind him a few paces, also running, was a boy. Conan guessed the boy's age at perhaps twelve winters, and he, too, was dressed in no more than a simple wrap of cloth about his loins.

Conan watched, intrigued, as the man leaped high into the air and came down near the end of the tree limb. That far out, the branch was very thin indeed, and it bent under the man's weight. Surely he would fall . . . ?

But—no. The bent branch recoiled, and the man flew upward into the air, propelled by the springy wood, so that he soared briefly like a bird. Still rising, he tucked himself into a ball and somersaulted, flipping forward much like an acrobat Conan had seen at a fair as a boy.

The man opened from his tuck and extended his arms and hands. He caught a tree limb fully three spans higher than the one from which he had leaped, and spun around it. All of a single move, he twirled his legs up and in a heartbeat hung head down by the backs of his knees, body outstretched, arms extended again.

Under the man, the boy sprang, using the limb for thrust. He, too, tucked into a tight ball and spun, turning once, twice, snapping open, arms outstretched. The man and boy met sharply, palms on each other's wrists, and swung back and forth for a second until the man flexed and tossed the boy up and overhead to perch lightly on the limb. After a moment, the man pulled himself up to sit next to the boy.

"The man is Tair," Cheen said, "the boy Hok. My mother's second child and her youngest."

"Your brothers," Conan said.

"Aye."

"A dangerous game they play. What if Tair should miss catching the boy?"

"There are many branches between there and the ground," Cheen said, shrugging. "Hok would likely find one."

"And if he did not?"

"Life is full of risks, is it not?"

Conan nodded. "Aye." Not every Cimmerian reached adulthood, either. A hardy people, these.

"Come," Cheen said, "you have shared your food and drink with me, it is only right that I offer you the hospitality our poor tree can provide.

Kleg did not like being so far away from water, and he especially did not like this particular kind of land, the dry and sandy

region men called desert. True, he and his
brothers had only a short stretch of the desert
to cross, a finger of the land belonging to the
lizards. Were the Pili to discover Kleg and his
troop, they would no doubt be unhappy to the
point of a killing attack, but this strip of their
territory was far from the main concentration
of the foul-smelling reptiles and likely to be
unnoticed. And if not, well, too bad. He Who
Creates had ordered that Kleg go to the forest
folk's domain by the fastest route; a detour to
avoid all the Pili's lands would add two days to
the journey. He Who Creates was not to be
disobeyed. Those who dared to trifle with Him
usually lived only just long enough to regret it.

Kleg sat perched uncomfortably upon the
back of the scrat, a stupid, mean-spirited beast
with four thick stumpy legs, a hide like moss-
covered rock, and a tendency to bite anything
it could reach. Half again Kleg's own height,
they were grass-eaters, the scrats, and would
spend all their time feeding if allowed to do so;
they could, however, store vast quanties of fat
in the big humps they carried over their hindquarters, and could go weeks without eating or
drinking. Would that He Who Creates had
given the packbeasts a better disposition and a
body odor other than that of week-old dead
fish.

Kleg turned to look at his troop. A score of
his brother selkies followed his lead, many on
scrats, some on foot, and all looking as uncom-
fortable in this barren, dry land as Kleg him-

self felt. He would prefer to be in the cool waters of home, his body shifted into the smooth and powerful form that was his natural shape. Ah, to be long and sinuous with rows of sharp teeth to rend his prey, his fins cutting powerfully through the water, feeding, then chasing the willing females for other pleasures. . . .

You dream, Kleg. He Who Creates did not make you for your pleasure, but to serve. Maybe once you fetch this thing He desires, you may be allowed some measure of relaxation; until then, best you take care of your task. Recall what happens to those who fail Him.

Kleg shuddered at the memory of the last Prime Brother. He Who Creates had set the Prime to some chore and the Prime had failed. When He Who Creates had finished with the Prime, the bits and pieces that remained had been fed to the scavengers. Horribly, even those scraps had seemed aware, wanting to scream, right up until they were consumed.

No, dream of swimming the dark waters *after* you achieve your goal, Kleg. Not before.

In the deep rock of the Pili's main cave, Rayk hissed at Thayla, his queen and mate. "Witch! What would you have of me?"

The Queen of the Pili reclined on a mound of furred cushions, her pale blue skin bare save for a gossamer gown of translucent red. Long ago, the Pili had been scaled, but after a million years of change, they could pass for men in dim light. They had no hair, their ears were somewhat smaller, but their blood was warm and they bore their young alive and nursed them as did mammals. Thayla's shape was that of a woman, her hips wide, her breasts heavy and full, and the thinness of her lips and the catlike pupils of her eyes did not detract from her exotic beauty.

Thayla smiled. "Why, I would have you do nothing, husband and King. The same as you always do." She watched him fume, his anger growing. Thayla knew precisely how to enrage Rayk. He was the strongest of the Pili, the fastest runner, without fear when facing an enemy, but in her hands, he was as a child.

"Thayla—"

"No, husband, you are right. The Tree Folk are strong in their high perches. Of course, had we the Talisman of the Forest, we, too, could fill our desert with lush growth and no longer have to scratch out a bare living."

"You lie on your cushions wrapped in the finest silks and talk about scratching out a bare living?"

"I am queen," she said. "Luxury is my right. Others of us are not so fortunate."

"And they would be less fortunate still were I to have them slaughtered under the big trees for your ambition."

"Surely there must be another way."

"Surely there must, but no Pili has discovered it in a thousand years."

"And would not the bards sing your glory

forever were you the one to devise such a way?"

He stood there staring at the tapestry woven by the Seventh Queen of the Pili more than twelve centuries past. The cloth painting showed the legendary Stak, the First King, leading a great army of Pili against humans in the Battle of Aranza. The bards still sang of the battle, in which men were driven from the Pili kingdom. Alas, that was long ago, and the numbers of the Pili had decreased even as those of men had grown. Now, only a few hundred of the Pili remained.

"Aye," Rayk finally said. "With such a magical device, we could move to the middle of the Great Desert, far from the reach of men, and regain our former strength."

"Well, then," Thayla said, "perhaps we can devise such a plan together, you and I."

She shifted her legs, allowing the red silk to fall away, revealing her body to Reyk. She smiled, and this one was of invitation and not scorn.

Reyk took a deep breath and released it, then moved toward her. "Perhaps," he said. His voice was little more than a whisper when he said, "You are a Paphian witch."

She laughed. "Aye, husband, come to your whore."

There was nothing humble about the feast spread before Conan. Upon a platform higher in the tree lay fruits, meats, a kind of bread, cheeses, and several wooden jars of wine. Steam rose from the cooked foods, and as Conan ate, he remarked on this to Cheen. "I would think fire a danger here."

"We floor our fireplaces with stone, as do ground dwellers. The wood of our trees is living, and therefore less likely to burn than the dead and dry timbers used for houses upon the earth."

Conan chewed on a bite of bread, then washed it down with a gulp of red wine. That made sense. "So, your people stay in the trees all the time?"

"Only most of the time. It is a rite of passage among us to descend to the ground for testing. And there are certain plants for medicines, materials such as stone and so forth, that must be gathered. Most of what we need is provided by the trees. We are content with our lot."

"How did these giant trees come to be?"

Cheen looked away, then back at Conan. "They have always been here," she said.

Something changed in her voice as she said this, and Conan knew she was lying. Some secret connected to the tree dwellers' homes. Ah, well. It was not his business. He would eat and rest and be on his way.

Shadizar awaited.

THREE

Abruptly, Dimma became solid.

It came upon him unexpectedly as always, and it had been years since he'd worn the flesh, so for a brief moment, he was overwhelmed with the sensations that arrived. He felt a coolness on his skin, a heaviness as vapor froze into muscle and bone and coursing blood, and even the itch on one arm was welcome. He was a man again!

There in his throne room, Dimma shouted for his selkie guards. They came on the run. There was no way to predict how long it would last, his return to real substance, and he knew he wanted to experience as many pleasures of the flesh as possible, as soon as possible.

"Bring me food, anything with taste! Call the witch woman Seg to me, hurry! A chamber pot! My meridian needles! Move! Now!"

The selkies sprinted to comply. They had been drilled in this exercise dozens of times, so that not an instant would be lost should Dimma coalesce from his normal state into that which he had once been.

As his servants rushed to obey him, Dimma stood and stretched, feeling the crackle of cartilage in his joints, the fibers of muscles throughout his form. Ah, this was bliss! His legs quivered at the unaccustomed weight upon them, his feet gloried in the coldness of the floor beneath them, he was aware of every inch of himself, of the air he breathed, the pull of the earth, the sounds of his heart pumping blood through his vessels. Gods, no man better appreciated his body than did Dimma in that moment.

A selkie rushed in carrying a tray piled high with steaming fish, a haunch of some denizen of the Sargasso, some greenish red fruit. For being the first to bring Dimma such a treat, the Mist Mage would reward the selkie with anything in his power to grant. Dimma grabbed at the food with both hands and savagely bit into whatever was topmost.

The scent of it nearly took his head off; the taste of fish brought tears it was so good.

The selkie stood holding the tray as Dimma grabbed at the contents and thrust hands full toward his mouth. The texture, the taste, the heat, the smell!

A second selkie arrived with Dimma's meridian needles, and the Mist Mage turned from the food, grease running down his chin, and snatched the *po* needle up and jammed it into his wrist, interrupting the flow of *see* energy in the invisible channel, causing a flowering of hot pain that raced through him. Even to feel pain again was a joy!

Seg arrived in the chamber, naked save for a hastily thrown-on cloak of sealskin. "To me, quickly!" Dimma ordered.

The witch started to shrug away the cloak.

"Leave it! I would touch it and you together."

Seg complied. He had not been able to lie with her for twenty years, but she was no less beautiful now than she had been then: her skin was ivory, her hair a raven's wing, her breasts and thighs and womanhood lush and inviting.

"Hurry," he said. The last time, he had become mist while with Seg, before he could accomplish what he set out to do. "Hurry!" he said as he pulled her toward him. By all the Gods, she felt so *good!* They fell to the floor together.

Prudently, the selkies looked away.

Kleg stopped his troops a few hours away from the Tree Folk's grove. They had passed a band of the Pili's hunting beasts, those nasty upright reptiles, only a short way back, but the dogs had been few in number and had declined to offer the selkie group any resistance. Doubtless they rushed to report the passage to their masters, but by the time that happened, the selkies were long out of Pili territory.

One problem was solved, but the major one remained: how were they to obtain the talisman He Who Creates desired? It was, Kleg knew, the most holy of the Tree Folk's relics, and they were not apt to part with it willingly. Kleg could have fielded an army ten times the number of the band he had brought, but he also knew that such an effort would have been pointless. The trees were too well fortified to storm by main force. The last time they tried a direct attack had been a disaster.

No, this called for guile, and he had only brought enough help to give the Tree Folk something upon which to focus while he worked out a means to obtain by subterfuge that which he must have. Kleg had not risen to be Prime due to a lack of wits. There had to be a way, and he would find it. Else he would no longer be Prime—or anything else. Such a spur provided him with excellent motivation. Achieve or die, that was the whole of it.

Kleg looked into the distant valley. He had several ideas; time, then, to winnow them and see what remained.

Cheen went off to make preparations for a ceremony scheduled for that night, leaving Conan in the company of her brothers, Tair and Hok. Their meeting had been amicable enough, though Conan was more than a little amused at the puffery of both the older and younger males.

"Ah, the giant barbarian of which I have

heard," Tair said. Standing next to him, Conan realized how small the man was; he barely reached the center of Conan's chest in height; he was shorter than Cheen by half a handspan. "I myself am the largest among the Tree Folk, both in what you see and what is covered." He dropped a hand to his breechcloth and winked at Conan.

"I shall leave you men to your lies," Cheen said.

After she departed, Tair and Hok took Conan on a tour of the trees. Each was linked to at least one other, Tair said, by vine bridges, so that one could move from one side of the grove to the other without difficulty. He, Tair, had personally built the highest and best of the bridges, with, he admitted, some small help from insignificant others.

Conan grinned. The bragging was so overt that it was not offensive. Tair could not open his mouth without crowing, and the boy Hok strived mightily to emulate his older brother.

"You saw my spring dance?" the boy said. "Tair says I am the best of all my age and better than many who are winters older, and it must be so for him to say it."

Conan nodded and tried not to laugh.

As they wended their way through the branches and across the bridges, Conan saw that indeed this was an entire village amongst the boughs, lacking little, if anything, that a similar town on the ground would have. Here, leaf-eating creatures were penned in small corrals; there, small gardens grew from dirt carefully mounded on thick tree limbs; over there, a platform large enough to hold fifty people was built and centered around one of the trees. Only such giants of the forest would support so much activity, but the Tree Folk had adapted themselves to a life in the air quite well. In Cimmeria, Crom lived under a mountain. What manner of gods would a tree people worship?

The three came to a bridge upon which there were four men. A dead limb had apparently fallen from some height, landing upon the bridge, and the angle of it made passage difficult. The four men were attempting to remove the obstruction, without apparent success. The limb was as thick as Conan's thigh and quite long, and the bridge was bent low under the weight.

"I am the strongest in the grove," Tair said. "I shall show these weaklings how a man moves a twig." He puffed up his chest and walked to where the four men were. There was a brief exchange, which became rather heated. Apparently the four did not wish for Tair to move the limb, thereby making them look ineffectual. Conan grinned.

After a moment, though, Tair squatted next to the branch and made as if to lift it. To his credit, he was able to move it slightly upward, but even as he sputtered and strained, it was apparent to Conan that the little man did not have the required strength.

Conan moved to where Tair grunted and heaved at the limb. "Heavy?" Conan said.

Tair desisted from his labor. "Indeed. If I cannot move it, no man among us can."

"Let me try."

"You are large, but size does not always mean strength."

"True."

"Still, you may try."

Conan took a wide stance and gripped the limb. He strained as his mighty legs began to straighten, and he felt the weight and knew he could lift the branch, albeit not easily. The weight began to move, then Conan glanced at Tair, and saw the man's worried frown. It came to Conan suddenly that if he managed the task, then Tair would no longer be the strongest man in the trees.

Conan considered it for a moment. He could move the branch and such would make him admired for his power by most, but Tair would suffer a loss of pride. And since such things were so highly valued among these men, Conan decided upon a second course of action.

The big Cimmerian relaxed and the branch settled. He saw a look of relief pass over Tair's features. "It is very heavy," Conan said.

Tair nodded.

"Those four could not move it, nor could you. And you have seen what I have done."

Tair said, "Aye."

"Perhaps the two of us can do what the four of them could not?"

The little man grinned. "Surely so."

Tair moved to stand next to Conan, and the two of them heaved upward against the branch. Conan took care not to lift too much, so that Tair felt his share of the weight. The dead branch came up and flipped over the side of the bridge to crash to the ground far below. The bridge sprang upward at the loss of weight, but none on it had trouble maintaining his footing.

Tair turned to the four. "See what men with *real* strength can do? This is Conan from the top of the world, and he is *my* friend!"

Tair slapped Conan on the back, and they and Hok proceeded upon their explorations.

Conan knew he had made a friend and not an enemy by his action, and he felt good for having done so.

Thayla moved from her pile of furred cushions where her husband slept the sleep of exhaustion. She smiled to herself as she went to see the root witch for a potion that would ensure she did not conceive from her just-finished activity with Rayk. Now was not the time to be great with child. No, soon her ambition to be queen of much more than a patch of scrub desert would begin to realize itself, and she needed to be able to guide that endeavor without any complications. There was much out there in the world that she would enjoy; Thayla would not be content to lie back and miss all the pleasures that power had to offer her. She had developed a liking for the forbidden and she would indulge herself more in it. One pleasure in particular fascinated her.

When the occasional human was captured, it meant for the Pili a feast. There was no taste to compare with manflesh, properly prepared, and all the Pili relished such treats. But sometimes, before the captives were cooked and eaten, they were kept alive for a time, to be fattened or flavored by special diets. And as queen, Thayla had access to these captives.

The idea at first had repelled her, but over time, she came to see certain desires as being her right. Rayk did not know, of course; only few of her trusted servants knew, but thrice, Thayla had taken her pleasure with human men in the same way she had just taken it with her husband. Such a thing was forbidden by Pili law, but she was, after all, queen, and in her mind, above the laws. Human men were different from Pili males, they smelled differently, acted differently, and they were ... larger in certain areas. Considerably so. Her first encounter with an aroused man had amazed her. She had not thought it possible to manage him, but she had, and she had found the sensation more pleasurable than ever it had been with Rayk, or any of the other Pili she sometimes took as lovers.

Alas, human captives were few and far between. Most of that race either did not know the Pili existed, or they had sense enough to avoid Pili territory. But if the Pili could grow in numbers, if they could find a place wherein they would not be bothered until they could become strong again, why, then, they could venture forth to ensnare unwary humans with more frequency. It would please her greatly should this come to pass, and she was just the person to manipulate it into happening. Rayk was strong and brutal, but he was a fool; she was the power behind him, and with sufficient prodding, he would do as she wished. He always had, and she had no intention of being thwarted in this desire.

As she approached the root witch's cave, Thayla smiled again. Life was easy for those who knew how to live it.

FOUR

Night stole into the valley like a master thief and draped her ebon and starry cloak over the giant trees. The sounds of chittering birds and insects formed a shifting web in the dark foliage, and torches guttered in their holders around the large platform Conan had seen earlier.

Cheen had invited him to the ceremony—there was to be a feast and plenty of wine—and Conan, never one to turn down a celebration, agreed to attend. He could return to his journey in the morning.

Only the leaders of each tree and their spouses would be allowed to partake of the potion Cheen had created this time, she told Conan. Eventually all of the Tree Folk would have their chance, but due to the scarcity of the ingredients, only small numbers could enjoy the Seeings at each ceremony.

When they arrived at the platform, at least thirty or forty people were already there, with others occupying a smaller platform nearby. Some of the celebrants sang, low and droning melodies, accompanied by musicians on drums and with wooden flutes. Conan noticed a number of coils of thin rope stacked near one edge of the platform, but before he could ask about these, Cheen said, "I must go to honor my mother. Will you be all right alone?"

Conan laughed. "The day a Cimmerian cannot manage to survive a friendly celebration will be the day the sun ceases to shine."

With Cheen vanished into the crowd, Conan wandered to a large table replete with food and drink. He sampled various roasted meats, tasted several wines, and decided that the Tree Folk were adept at both cooking and vintnery.

There was a large wooden bowl of dark red wine in the center of the table that was as good as any Conan had ever had. He dipped one of the wooden cups with the ornately carved handles into the wine for a second serving, and decided that there certainly must be worse places for a man to spend his time than in these trees.

A short while later, Cheen returned to find Conan. He was feeling extraordinarily good, and he grinned widely at her.

"The ceremony is about to begin," she said. "Are you certain you do not wish to partake?"

"Thank you, but nay. Your people set a fine table, Cheen, and I have sated myself with both food and wine. That dark wine is especially potent."

"Dark wine?"

"In the large wooden bowl." Conan waved at the table behind him.

"You drank from that bowl?"

"Aye. Two cups' worth. I was sorely tempted to have more, so good was it, but I thought not to be greedy."

"Who is your god, Conan?"

"My god? Why, Crom the Warrior, who lives under the Mountain of Heroes. Why do you ask?"

She laid one hand on his solid shoulder and smiled at him. "Because the wine in the sacred bowl from which you drank is the same in which the Seeing medicine was mixed."

That took a moment to sink into Conan's consciousness. "What?"

"If the potion works for you as it does for us, you shall have an opportunity to see your god shortly."

Conan stared at her. "Is there an antidote for your potion?"

"I am afraid not."

Conan considered that for a moment. To see Crom? He was not at all certain that he desired to do that.

Kleg lay hidden by the night only a few paces away from one of the large trees, considering his options. There appeared to be some kind of ritual going on in the trees; a large number of the Tree Folk sang and danced on a large platform twenty times his height above the ground. His own troops rested less than half an hour behind him. The talisman he sought was, he knew, in this very tree. The capture and torture of one of the residents had revealed this knowledge sometime past, and the revelry above might well play into Kleg's hands. Under the dark's helpful cover, a few of the selkies might ascend the trunk of the giant tree, using the special gloves and boots made of shark-brother's hide and teeth. While a distraction on the other side of the grove drew their attention, he could try for the prize. Probably some of the guards would be sober, but with that many drunks wandering around, surely their vigilance might be lax?

Abruptly, Kleg decided. Yes. He would take two of his brothers with him and the rest would raise a din elsewhere once he and his two soldiers reached a position from which they could strike at their goal.

Kleg hurried back through the dark toward his hidden troops. The night was young, and in an hour or two, they could be ready to move.

Conan awoke suddenly. His head hurt, and he felt muzzy. He sat up. What had happened ... ?

Ah. He recalled. That dark wine, the potion ...

He observed his surroundings. He was on the platform, and there were perhaps two dozen of the Tree Folk lying asleep or sitting groggily around him; night still held sway, and Conan could not say how long he had slept. Apparently Cheen's potion did not affect Cimmerians in the same manner as it did her people. Just as well—

"Ho, Conan!" The voice was loud, impossibly deep, vibrant with power, alive with force.

Conan turned.

Standing on the end of the platform was a giant of a man, half again Conan's height, thickly muscled, clad in fur boots and a wolfskin codpiece, his bare chest gleaming with oil in the flickering light of the dimming torches. The man had a full beard, his teeth shining whitely in a huge smile, and upon his dark red hair he wore an ornate bronze helmet bearing a pair of long and curved horns. Here was a warrior, no doubt of it, a man to inspire awe.

Conan got to his feet. "Who calls Conan?"

The giant laughed. "Do you not recognize me?"

Conan felt a fluttery sensation in his bowels, as if something alive were being kept captive there and had suddenly grown most unhappy about it. Surely it could not be? In that moment, however, he felt certain that indeed it was.

"Crom," he said, his voice very soft.

"In the flesh, boy. Come to see what I have made."

Conan licked suddenly dry lips. One did not meet a god every day. "What would you have of me?"

"Why, nothing, boy. You have nothing to offer. You are a weakling."

Anger welled in Conan, and the dullness in his smoldering blue eyes vanished, growing preternaturally sharp. "No man calls Conan a weakling!"

"No man has, fool."

Conan removed his sword and sheath from his belt and set it upon the platform.

"What think you are doing now?" Crom asked.

Conan flexed his hands, rolled his shoulders to loosen them, and took a step forward. "I would show you that you are in error," Conan said.

Crom laughed again. "You would grapple with me? You would dare wrestle a *god?*"

"Aye. There is little a Cimmerian will not dare."

"I think perhaps I gave you too much bravery and not enough wits."

"Perhaps." Conan continued stalking toward the giant.

"Very well, then, Conan of Fooleria. Come and pit your strength against mine."

Conan nodded. Certainly there were worse ways to die than wrestling with your god; there could hardly be a harder challenge. Not that he intended to lose.

Conan gathered his muscles for a leap, took two more quick steps, and leaped for Crom—

And jumped right off the platform into empty air.

Conan had time to hear Crom laugh and see him vanish as he fell toward the ground, so far below as to be invisible in the night. He also had time to remember that Crom was supposedly most fond of jesting and that this joke was certainly well played upon Conan....

Kleg directed the bulk of his force to a position some distance away from the target tree. He handed the subleader a stubby candle protected from stray breezes by a thin, hollow crystal open at the top and bottom. The small light within was hidden by a cover of ray hide. "When the flame reaches the second ring, start your attack. Make a lot of noise, bang shields and spears together, start little fires, I care not, only be certain to attract a lot of attention. Wait until the flame touches the second ring so that we shall have time to reach our goal."

"As you command, Prime."

With his two strongest troopers, Kleg returned to the target, moving with great care. The whole of his force wore dark clothing over their already-dark skin, and the chances of being seen were slight, at least until they were into the tree itself.

The three put on their shark-hide-and-teeth gloves and boots and began to climb. The sharp teeth bit into the smooth bark like claws, allowing them to inch their way upward. Once they attained the lower branches, it would go much faster.

Nearing the place where a guard stood on a

limb, Kleg had one of his troopers move around where he might be seen. Sure enough, the guard heard or saw something.

"Who's there? Is that you, Jaywo? I am not amused at your antics!" This was one of the males, a gruff-voiced and older one. When no answer came, the guard grew suspicous. "Jaywo? Answer!" The guard lifted the short spear and pointed it at the climbing selkie.

But before the guard could thrust downward, Kleg reached the branch behind the guard. Kleg pulled his knife, a razor-edged sliver of obsidian, and leaped upon the guard. A quick slash opened the guard's throat before he could cry out a warning, and a shove launched the dying man into the air. The noise of his landing was louder than Kleg had thought, but not so loud as to draw notice from above.

"Hurry," Kleg said. "We have but a short time."

The two selkies obeyed their leader, and all three moved quickly along the thick limb, angling upward.

Conan awoke with his head threatening to burst this time, and found himself dangling in midair by a rope around his left ankle. Even as he realized this, somebody started to haul him up toward the platform above.

Conan lifted himself and caught the rope with his hands so that he was upright, and he began to climb. It was but the work of a moment to reach the platform.

On the other end of the rope stood Cheen, Tair, and two other men. Tair said, "By the great Green One, you are as heavy as that branch we moved."

Conan was confused. "How came I to be down there? I recall seeing—seeing . . . Crom. We—he—I offered to wrestle him."

Cheen said, "The potion sometimes causes disorientation. We all wear safe lines once the ceremony begins." She pointed at her ankle.

Indeed, all of the people wore such ropes, at least the ones Conan could see. Those coils he had seen earlier. That was what they were for. Wise.

"Since you are a stranger to our ways, I put the line on for you while you slept."

"I am in your debt," Conan said.

"And was your visit with your god a good one?"

"It was . . . instructive," Conan said. Aye. One had best be wary of challenging a god, be he real or an illusion. Especially one with a sense of humor as had Crom.

To his left, someone on the ground began yelling. A number of them, did Conan's ears not lie, making quite a racket.

"What . . . ?" he began.

"Intruders in the grove!" Cheen said. "We are under attack. It must be the selkies again!"

"Selkies?"

"To arms!" Tair yelled. "To arms!"

Conan saw his sword, lying where he had left it. He hurried toward it. He did not know who or what selkies were, but if there was fighting to be done, he knew well how to swing a blade.

Kleg watched as the people on the platform, now below his position, began to stream toward the sound of his troops. There was one who did not seem to belong here, a large and bulky man with square-cut black hair and a large sword, but that was of no import now. The talisman he sought was only a few steps away, past two female guards armed with spears.

Kleg nodded to his two selkies. They each drew a pair of obsidian knives and rushed along the narrow branch one behind the other.

The two guards caught sight of the approaching selkies. One of them threw her spear; the weapon's point pierced the throat of the first of his selkies. The trooper fell wordlessly, but even as he did, he threw both of his knives. His dying action served only to wound one of the guards, but it was enough so that the second selkie could get close enough to launch himself at the two women. The selkie and one of the women fell; she screamed all the way down.

The second woman managed to catch the limb with one hand, but her action was wasted, for Kleg arrived and stamped on her fingers with his toothed boot. She lost her grip and fell.

Kleg was at the entrance to the building and he used his blade to slice open the ceremonial knot binding the door closed.

Inside was a single chest, also bound with a

special knot, and his blade made short work of it as well. He opened the chest and in the dim light saw the talisman.

It was a seed, hard and eye-shaped, the size of a small apple, warm and moist to his touch. He looked at it for a second, then jammed it into his belt pouch and hurried from the chamber. He had lost two selkies and he might lose others when they were attacked from the trees, but it did not matter. He had what he had come for!

As Kleg was letting down the ladder rope for his descent, he caught sight of a small form darting along a branch. He had been seen.

Quickly, Kleg climbed and hid behind an outcropping of foilage. After a moment, one of the males, a small one, scooted along the branch just in front of him. Kleg reached out and clouted the boy with the butt of his knife, knocking him senseless. He started to cut the boy's throat, then stopped. No. He would take the boy along. There might be something to learn from interrogating him; besides, should they encounter the Pili on their return home, the boy might be made to serve other purposes. The Pili, he knew, were more than passing fond of eating human flesh. Perhaps they could buy safe passage with such a tidbit.

Kleg was very strong compared to a man, and shouldering the boy's weight and climbing down the vine was not difficult in the least.

Once on the ground, he hurried to the prearranged meeting place where he would be joined by his troops.

He had accomplished his ordered task and he was jubilant. It had almost been too easy, but he was not one to tempt fate by dwelling on that thought.

FIVE

Conan followed Tair, winding through the trees toward the sounds of battle. Several times the big Cimmerian almost lost his balance on some of the smaller limbs, but each time managed to recover in time to maintain the chase. Along their route other armed men and women joined the procession. After a final short sprint, they arrived at the tree edging the far end of the grove.

The members of the besieged tree had dropped dozens of flaming balls of pitch, so that the scene below them was easily viewed. Conan saw perhaps a dozen shadowy shapes darting about, and their behavior seemed more than passing strange. They made much noise, the attackers, screaming and slinging stones and hurling spears upward, but there seemed to be much ado about little. At first, those below looked to be men, but as Conan drew nearer, he was able to detect an inhuman aspect to their shape and movements. They were the right size and general shape, they had faces and hands and yelled in manlike tones, but they were somehow alien. Selkies, Tair had called them.

Tair slid to a stop on a broad limb and leaned forward, his spear held high and ready to cast. But he held the throw, hesitating.

Conan came to stand next to him. The air was heavy with the sharp stench of the sputtering pitch below. He looked at Tair.

"What are they doing?" Tair said. "Have they gone mad?"

Indeed, Conan thought. Those in the trees were in no danger from those capering below. In fact, several of the selkies lay sprawled on the ground, outlined in flickering yellow from the burning resin globs lying about, Tree Folk spears sprouting like stiff weeds from their corpses. "A diversion?" Conan offered.

"Aye." Tair nodded. "But—from what are they diverting us?"

"Perhaps we should capture one and ask it."

"A good idea, Conan."

Tair moved to a coil of climbing vine and kicked it over the edge of the branch. He moved down the rope even before it completely stretched out, and Conan had never seen a man climb with such speed; a spider could have done it no better on his own line of webbing.

Conan immediately followed Tair down the cable of plaited vine.

If the selkies took any notice of Tair and Conan, they gave no sign, but as Conan neared two spans above the ground, the yelling attackers abruptly turned and squinted into the darkness.

Conan leaped the final distance, pulled his sword forth with a rasp of leather and a ring of tempered iron, and charged after Tair, who pursued the suddenly fleeing selkies. The tree dweller might be a faster climber, but Conan's long and powerful legs gave him the edge on the ground. In two heartbeats, the Cimmerian passed Tair and began gaining on the retreating selkies. Conan had time to wonder why the attackers fled. Surely one small tree dweller and one somewhat larger Cimmerian could not have frightened them so badly? Most odd.

That was something to worry over later, though. Conan began to overtake the selkie nearest the rear of the running group, and he had to decide how best to stop the straggler without killing him. A sword thrust to one leg? Aye, that would do it.

The starlight reflected from the blued iron blade as the running man took aim at the intended target and prepared to strike—

At that moment, however, the fleeing selkie must have sensed his danger. Whether he heard Conan's thudding footsteps or caught some peripheral movement or detected his pursuer with some sense unknown to men, it mattered not, for he glanced over his shoulder, saw Conan, and dodged sharply just as Conan jabbed with the point of his heavy sword.

The intended thrust missed its mark, and the lack of expected resistance off-balanced Conan the slightest bit. In itself this would have been of little consequence; however, at that precise moment a gnarled root loomed from the dark ground, Conan's bare foot connected with the root, and he tripped. Such was the Cimmerian's momentum that he took to the air, launched from the earth in a headlong dive. Conan uttered a curse he had first heard his father speak when once the smith had accidentally struck his hand with a forge hammer.

Fortune smiled upon the endangered selkie, only to turn its back with a frown an instant later. The selkie saw Conan's mishap, must have thought it an intentional leap, and dodged again. Alas for the selkie, he mistook the angle of his pursuer's flight and instead of leaving Conan's path, he shifted the wrong way; realizing his error, the selkie tried to twist away, succeeding only in stopping cold.

Conan smashed into the startled selkie with all of his not inconsiderable weight, stretching the creature out and slamming him facedown into the ground with the man on his back. The two slid for perhaps three spans, the Cimmerian youth riding the figure beneath him as a boy rides a sled across new snow.

The other selkies quickly gained the cover of night and disappeared.

Tair arrived a moment later and skidded to a stop. "I am the best spring dancer in the trees," he said as Conan stood, "but you must teach me that leap, I have never seen anything quite like it."

Conan looked down at the unconscious selkie, then at Tair. He had the presence of mind to shrug. "That? That was nothing, a child's trick where I come from."

"Shall we take this one back and question him?"

"Aye," Conan began.

He was interrupted by the sound of approaching footfalls. Conan spun away from the downed selkie, sword held ready, but it was a contingent from the trees and not the selkie's comrades.

"The sacred Seed!" one of the men yelled. "They have stolen the sacred Seed!"

Back at the tree in which the god-seeing ceremony had been held, Conan listened as Cheen explained.

"The trees of our grove are the mightiest in all the world," she said, "but it was not always so. Twenty generations past, the most powerful of our medicine women created a spell that caused normal trees to grow thrice or more times their usual size."

Conan nodded, but did not speak. He looked at the empty chest at her feet.

"But it was not enough that they should grow. The ground here cannot provide enough nourishment for the roots of so many trees such as ours. So the medicine woman—she was known as Jinde—wove another spell, which she invested in a special seed. It gives great energy to any plants near it."

Magic. A thing not at all to Conan's liking. It seemed to be everywhere he went, and he would avoid dealing with it, given a choice.

"Without the seed," Cheen continued, "our trees will soon wither and die."

Well. A sad fate, but not really Conan's concern. Best to leave magic to those who wanted to deal with it.

Before Cheen could continue, Tair came running toward them. "Have you seen Hok?" he said, all out of breath.

"No," Cheen answered. She looked at Conan.

"Not since before the ceremony," he said.

"He should be in the boys' hut," Cheen said.

Tair nodded. "Aye, he should be, but he is not."

"Have the call drum sounded. He is probably up and wandering about because of all the excitement," she said.

But when the last echoes of the drum faded, the boy Hok did not respond, and a search of every tree also failed to turn him up. When the hunt had been completed, Cheen's face was a mix of rage and sorrow as she said, "Along with the life of our grove, the selkies have stolen my youngest brother!"

The sun blazed and beat upon the heads of the selkies as they trudged across the isthmus of dry sand belonging to the Pili. Kleg would feel much better once they had achieved the coolness of the distant mountains, both for reasons of comfort and of safety. Good fortune had traveled with them during the outward-bound journey and he would have such luck continue as they returned home with their master's prize.

It was not to be. From behind a tall hillock of sand and scrubby growth ahead, a troop of Pili emerged, armed with their long dart slingers and prepared for battle.

Kleg counted the lizard men and saw that they numbered only slightly more than his own band. He called his selkies to a halt.

Normally, a group such as Kleg's would be attacked immediately; however, the Pili seemed in no great hurry to begin the fight that would surely end with much death on both sides. They, too, stopped and waited. Kleg took this as a good sign.

After a few moments, one of the Pili stepped forward. From the bright red sash he wore wrapped around his middle, Kleg assumed he was the leader. It was difficult to say, since the Pili all looked alike to him. The single Pili strode toward the selkies.

One of Kleg's troopers raised a spear, but Kleg waved one hand at him. "Nay, hold," he said. "Perhaps we might come to some accommodation." Kleg stepped forward and walked toward the approaching lizard man. When they were two spans apart, both stopped.

"You trespass on Pili territory," the lizard man said. His accent was harsh, but his command of the common tongue was adequate for normal conversation.

Kleg did not bother to try and deny it. "Aye. My master, He Who Creates, has bid me to achieve His business with haste; to go around would cost two days."

"Attempting to cross will surely cost you much more. My master, the Lord High King Rayk, has charged *me* with protecting his domain from unauthorized trespass."

"It seems we are at an impasse then."

"So it seems. We outnumber you."

"Indeed, but by a small margin. If we fight, most of us will likely die on both sides."

"True. It is unfortunate, but not to be helped." The lizard man turned to walk back to his troops.

"But hold a moment," Kleg said. "Perhaps there is a way around this dilemma."

The lizard man stopped. "I am listening."

"What if there were a way for our passage to be authorized?"

"Hardly likely."

"Yet you could grant us crossing were there a compelling reason?"

"It is within the realm of possibility."

Kleg spoke rapidly in true selkie speech, a liquid whistling that the lizard man could not possibly understand. One of Kleg's troop dismounted from his packbeast and approached, carrying a large leather sack over his shoulder.

The Pili's hand drifted toward the knife at his belt.

"Nay, friend, there is no treachery here. Bide a moment."

The selkie with the sack placed it upon the ground and stood away.

"I am given to understand that the Pili have a most interesting diet at times."

"Not for fishman flesh, which is exceedingly vile," the lizard man said.

Kleg nodded. He knew as much and was also exceedingly glad of it. "But behold." He bent and opened the sack, then upended it, to reveal the still-unconscious boy kidnapped from the trees.

The Pili's slit eyes widened. "Ah. A human."

"Indeed. If truth must be known, we have no great use for him ourselves. Perhaps you would take him off our hands?"

The lizard man blinked and appeared to consider this. "In exchange for allowing you to pass unmolested."

"That had occurred to me, yes."

"He is not very large, the human."

"True, but the only one we happen to have at the moment. And consider the alternative. Your men and mine will fight bravely and many will die. You may win, but it will be a costly victory at best. If you manage to survive to return to your king only to report most of your troop has been slain, surely that will not be happy news?"

"Surely not."

"If, on the other hand, you return with this nice tender young boy for the communal pot, would that not reflect more honor upon you?"

The Pili glanced over his shoulder at his band, then back down at the boy. "There is some merit in that which you speak," the lizard man finally said. "Of course, the Pili are fierce warriors and we could probably slay you and take the boy anyway."

"The bravery of the Pili has never been in question," Kleg said. "Still, it would not be an easy task."

The lizard man nodded. "Aye, the fishmen are not inconsiderable opponents." He looked up from the boy and stretched his lips in a horrible grimace. At first, Kleg took this to be a threat, then he realized it was in fact a smile.

"We of the Pili are feeling benevolent this day, and in honor of the approaching Moon Festival, have decided to allow safe passage to the band of fishmen who wandered onto our territory accidentally."

"You are generous and wise," Kleg said.

"So it has been said before."

"If ever you should happen to be in my land, be certain to ask after me."

"Indeed."

The deal was done, and cheap at the price, Kleg figured. Nothing stood between him and his goal now, save a few days of uneventful travel. He Who Creates would be most pleased.

Six

Dimma lifted to his lip a carved gold cup of fine wine produced by the famed Aquilonian winemakers; indeed, the region bordering the Tyborg River just south of Shamar might well be the source of the most exquisite wines in the world, and this particular vintage was the best of the best. It had taken only a few hours before the newness of being flesh again had allowed just any sensation to be a wonder; now, Dimma required a higher stimulation, such as this rare and valuable wine. He smiled as he inhaled the fragrance of it, anticipating the smoothness of it on his palate.

Alas, it was not to be. Even as he tilted the gold cup, he felt the sense of cold that some-times presaged his change.

"No!"

The cup fell. He had not dropped it, only

ceased being able to hold it. Even as the falling container passed through his lap to splash on the throne under him, Dimma reaped the fruit of a dying wizard's curse, becoming no more solid than smoke.

He raged, hurling curses of his own after the centuries-dead wizard of Koth, hoping his epithets would seek out and find the soul of his tormentor no matter how deep the pit of Gehanna he inhabited. Dimma called upon the pox of poxes, the blackest of evil demons, the hate of every major and minor god to smite his old enemy.

He found himself drifting a few steps away from his throne and stopped his imprecations. Once again, he was a disembodied voice, lacking that which most men took for granted. His curses gained him nothing. His hope lay in collecting the final ingredient for his cure. The other parts lay well guarded in the safest chamber of his castle, awaiting only the final talisman and the utterance of the spell, the words of which Dimma now knew as well as the back of his ghostly hand. He had said the words in his mind ten thousand times, practicing for the day when he could speak them aloud and remove this malediction at last.

Where are you, Kleg? Best hope that you have what I need, and best you hurry!

"What will they do with the boy?" Conan asked.

Tair, busy gathering supplies for a long trek,

said, "Kill him. That is not the question, only when and how. The selkies are thralls to the Mist Mage, the Abet Blasa, who lives in the great mountain lake six days from here. They have stolen our Seed, doubtless for some nefarious purpose, and our grove dies without it. As for my brother . . ." He shrugged. "We can only hope to catch them before they dispose of him."

Conan nodded, aware of the seriousness of Tair's intent. Not once had he bragged during his explanation.

"We could use another strong man," Tair said.

"Aye," said Cheen, coming up behind Tair, her own pack already loaded. "Your help would be welcome."

Conan considered it. Cheen had saved him from the dragon, though he had repaid that debt almost immediately. And they had offered him their hospitality, he had eaten their food and drunk their wine, albeit the latter had given him somewhat more adventure than he had anticipated. Such a courtesy did not demand his allegiance to the death, of course. Still, the memory of his own slavery when not much older than Hok was still strong in Conan. He hated slavers and child stealers.

"When do we leave?" Conan said.

The boy was too young for her usual ministrations, Thayla decided. Then again, he was young and therefore tender, and certainly his arrival could not be considered an ill fortune. A small feast before she sent her loutish husband off to seek the magic secret of the Tree Folk would not be unwelcome. Warriors might fight more wolfishly with empty bellies, but a taste of things to come might also spur the Pili expedition on to great effort. She had already convinced Rayk that once they began their oasis in the desert, such treats would be only a matter of time. The Pili were few in number and slow to breed; however, their advantage lay in reaching adulthood much faster than did the more numerous humans. Raise a Pili child and a human side by side and the Pili would be fully grown while the other was still learning to walk. That could be turned to their advantage, given time.

Stal, the commander of the troop that had returned bearing the boy, stood with Rayk, repeating—and doubtless embellishing—the story of how they had come by the human.

"—and even though we were outnumbered four to one by the fishmen, they were so fearful that they tendered the human and begged for our mercy. Since the Moon Festival is nearly upon us, and since they were so repentant over their error in blundering quite by accident onto our territory, I decided to spare them. After all, what is a festival without a feast?"

Rayk nodded and slapped Stal on the shoulder. "You have done well, Stal. I have no doubt you could have slaughtered the offending fishmen easily, but your actions showed a fine grasp of tactics. Better to feast than to be burying one's comrades."

Thayla rolled her eyes upward and looked away. Just like males, standing around congratulating themselves on how brave and mighty they were, doubtless lying about nearly all of it. Then again, Stal was a fair specimen of Pili male—he had made a few overtures in Thayla's direction—and she might one day, out of boredom, take him to her bed. He had ambition, this one, and might prove useful to her.

The human was in the cage built for such purposes, awake and watching his captors somewhat fearfully. Likely he knew his fate.

Thayla walked to the cage and smiled at the young captive. "Hungry?" she asked.

He did not respond.

"Do not worry, you shall be well fed. The Moon Festival is but four days hence, and until then, you shall have as much as you can eat. Would that we had captured you a moon or so past, though. Four days is hardly enough time to add much to your small frame."

She smiled again, and took a small pleasure as the boy shuddered. He knows, well enough.

But as Thayla turned away in a thin rustle of silk, a thought occurred to her. Why were the fishmen crossing her territory? They must have come from the grove of the Tree Folk, else how had they come by one of them as a captive?

The Queen of the Pili walked toward the king and Stal.

"Pardon, great warrior, but did the fishmen say what business they had with the Tree Folk?"

Stal looked at her, his gaze quickly but unobtrusively traversing her lush body. Rayk appeared to take no notice, but Thayla certainly did. He was hungry for her.

"No, my queen, they did not speak of this."

"What does it matter to us what the fishmen do?" Rayk interjected.

"Concerning the Tree Folk and certain plans you and I have discussed, my lord king, everything matters."

"Ask the boy," Rayk said. He laughed. "Perhaps *he* knows the minds of the fishmen."

It was meant as a joke, but Thayla spun, her silk flaring out to reveal her nude body under it to Stal, exactly as she intended. "I shall."

At the cage, she said, "Harken, boy. What do you know of the fishmen's business at your grove?"

The boy crouched at the far side of the cage, silent.

"Speak."

He said nothing.

Thayla considered this. Were you in his place, would you say anything, knowing your immediate future lay in a cooking pot as a meal for your captors? Decidedly not.

"Very well. Speak and you shall have your freedom."

Behind her, Rayk uttered a short curse and moved toward his queen. "Hold, Thayla!"

She waved at him impatiently. "Silence, husband."

The boy looked at the king, then back at Thayla. "Is this true? If I tell you, you shall let me go?"

"Upon the grave of my mother I so swear," Thayla said.

The boy blinked and appeared to think about it for a second. Then he said, "They stole the Seed," he said. "I saw one of them take it. I tried to follow him, but I was caught."

Thayla stared at the boy. The Seed. He must mean the Talisman of the Forest. How could it be possible that the fishmen could do what the Pili had failed to do for so long? "By the Great Dragon! Is this true?"

"Yes, mistress."

Thayla turned to glare at Stal. "You fool! You allowed the fishmen to pass carrying a great treasure!"

"Thayla—" Rayk began.

She turned her glare upon him but did not speak.

Rayk did not need her prompting, however. To Stal he said, "Assemble your troop. Full strength, take enough to offset the fishmen's numbers. I shall personally lead them after the fishmen. With luck, we can catch them before they attain the great lake." He turned toward Thayla as Stal scurried from the rocky chamber.

"You had better catch them," Thayla said. "If the magician of the lake gets his hands on that talisman, it is lost to us for certain."

"Mistress," came the boy's voice from the cage. "Did you forget your promise to free me?"

Thayla did not even bother to look at him when she spoke. "Do not be stupid, boy. You are not going anywhere."

"You swore an oath!"

"I lied. Take it up with your god when you see him. In four days."

Kleg had anticipated a quiet journey, but he had not figured on something no selkie had ever been able to predict: the weather.

Shortly after they left the desert behind and reached the foothills, a storm began brewing. Kleg could feel the moisture in the air and it was not unwelcome in one sense, but it would slow them some, should it continue to gather, and should it happen to move their way.

The storm did both. Purple-gray clouds built a tower toward the sun, mushrooming at the top into fleecy tatters. Lightning danced in the heart of the storm, and the rumble of some god's drums rolled over the mesa toward the selkies. A herald wind blew, the breeze full of dampness, and within a few minutes, the gray curtain sweeping toward them arrived. Fat drops splattered on the dry ground, kicking up tiny clouds of dust at first. When the full force of the storm flowed over them, the world turned dark and gray, visibility dropped to a few spans, and the stupid pack scrats obstinately stopped and refused to move, even under spear-point prods.

Kleg grinned up into the bowels of the storm. Well, if you cannot avoid it, you might as well enjoy it, he thought. The rain was so heavy you could almost Change and breathe it, and it was tempting to shift his form and lie at least partially submerged in one of the deepening puddles all around them. He would not, of course, but it was tempting.

They were on high enough ground, no risk of a flash flood, though some of the small streams they had crossed outbound would be swollen into rushing rivers by the rain. Crossing a river was hardly an obstacle to a selkie, and if the packbeast refused to swim, why, then, they could be dinner for their former riders after the Change. It would serve the damned things right, and it would be worth the walk the rest of the way home, Kleg decided. He Who Creates did not count such beasts generally, and would certainly not care about them when balanced against the talisman Kleg carried in his pouch. Hardly.

Smiling, Kleg enjoyed the rain.

The Tree Folk had two dozen armed members in its party, about equal numbers of men and women. More, they had some strange tracking beasts that looked to be big spotted cats, unlike any Conan had seen before. They kept the cats leashed, a dozen of them on thick leather straps, two or three per handler.

Cheen and Tair set a good pace, but it was no trouble for Conan to maintain; in fact, he offered to go ahead. Cimmerians might not climb as well as did these people, but they were second to none as trackers. Conan could easily see the signs of the selkie's passage, even on the shifting sandy ground of the Pili's territory.

Eager to rescue their brother and talisman, Cheen and Tair agreed with Conan's suggestion. He loped off easily, following the trail that might as well have been a road before him.

"Beware the Pili's dogs!" Cheen called out as Conan moved away from the band.

"Aye, I shall," Conan called back to her.

The Pili troop numbered nearly a hundred, and it was augmented by half that many of the dragon-like Korga. The Korga ranged ahead, on the trail of the fishmen, and the Pili followed them at very nearly a run. Thayla watched them depart. Her fool of a husband had better catch the blasted fishmen.

She smiled as she turned back toward the entrance to her chambers. Well, if they were gone more than a few days, they would miss the feast. Sad for them, but not for those who remained behind. Especially her; as Queen, she would get the best parts, including those normally reserved for the King. It was indeed an ill wind that blew no good at all. One had to take one's compensations where one could find them. And the thought of it made her mouth water.

SEVEN

Conan had gained half a day on the Tree Folk when he found the signs of a meeting between the selkies and another group. To the east, a line of storms thundered distantly, but the dry ground here held shallow impressions altered only slightly by wind and sun. From behind that sandy hillock had come a band whose footprints differed from those of the selkies. At first, they looked like man tracks, but a closer examination revealed subtle differences. Pili, Conan figured, since this was supposedly their territory.

The big Cimmerian quartered the area, with the sun baking his tanned skin darker all the while. Here, two members of the selkies had moved to meet a single footman from the Pili. One of the selkies had carried something heavy enough to make him sink deeper into the soft ground when he approached the meeting, but had not carried it away when he left. On the other hand, the Pili had left much deeper tracks when he had turned back toward his party. There was a depression in the earth, just there, where something smaller than a man but large enough to be a boy had been dropped. Whatever it was, the Pili had taken it.

Unschooled in civilized ways Conan might be, but he could read trail sign. The selkies had given something to the Pili here. According to what Cheen had told him as they began their trek, the selkies and Pili were not on friendly terms, as likely to fight when meeting as not, especially on Pili home ground.

Conan raised from his squat by the tracks. He looked toward the north, where the Pili tracks led. The lizard men ate human flesh, Cheen had said. Conan could imagine that a bargain might have been struck, with the boy Hok as some kind of bribe.

Which way should he go? The selkies' trail lay to the east, and they had taken both the magic Seed and the boy. But if the Pili now had Hok, he was possibly in more peril than before; like as not, the selkies would keep him until they returned to their master; the Pili, on the other hand, might eat him sooner.

Conan decided. The Seed would keep indefinitely, but the boy might not. He would go north.

Conan stripped a dry branch from one of the scrub plants, broke it into a number of parts, and made from it an arrow he laid on the ground, pointing after the Pili trail. Under this, he created a small stick figure meant to represent Hok. A second arrow indicated the selkie trail, and under this one, he formed an outline of a seed. When Cheen and Tair and the others reached here, they would know which way Conan had gone, and why. With luck, they would find the picture before the wind covered it with dust.

The big man took a long sip of water from the skin he carried over one shoulder, adjusted his sword belt, and started north.

The storm that delayed the selkies was but one of several, and while Kleg fretted at the delay, there was nothing to be done. A god might move the rain, but a selkie could do nothing but wait.

There were several ponds that had been shallow and scummy only hours before but now were quite deep. And as long as they were stuck here, Kleg finally decided it might as well be a pleasant stay.

"Bring one of the scrats," he ordered one of his selkies. He had to yell to be heard over the steady downpour. "Shove it off that rise into that lake."

"My Lord Prime?" the selkie began, puzzled.

Kleg smiled widely, showing many teeth. "Perhaps the brothers would enjoy a swim—with a bit of dinner included?"

The selkie mirrored Kleg's smile. "Yes, Prime, immediately!"

Thayla was returning from the kitchen, where she had been discussing the preparation of the uncoming Moon Festival feast, when she heard some kind of commotion outside. Could her husband have retrieved the magic talisman already?

The queen stopped a young female returning from the main entrance to the caves. "What is that noise outside?"

The female, naked save for a leather crotch strap, but too young for anything other than budding breasts and a distant promise of more, bowed and said, "The Korga, my lady."

"I thought the king took the Korga with him."

"Not all, my lady."

Thayla went to see for herself what the beasts were hissing and moaning about.

Outside, the desert wind blew warmly, but with a hint of moisture. It appeared to be raining to the east, but more than a little distance away. Rain here was a rarity; it did not happen more than once or twice every season, and not plentifully at that.

The Korga master stood yelling at six or seven of the man-sized and mostly stupid lizards, who dashed back and forth in their high-fenced yard excitedly.

"Silence, you ignorant beasts!"

The Korga master was an old Pili; he had

been old when, as a child, Thayla had first seen him, and he seemed unchanged in all that time. "What is it, Rawl?"

The old Pili shrugged. "I cannot say, my lady. The Korga smell something out there."

"What are you going to do about it?"

He shrugged again. "Nothing. The king told me to keep this bunch penned."

"The king is not here and I am. Release the Korga to go and chase whatever is bothering them so that we may have quiet here."

"By your command, Queen Thayla."

Rawl opened the gate to the pen and the Korga dashed out in that funny gait they had, their thick tails stuck out behind for balance as they ran. She did not much care for the things, and were it up to her, would keep none about the caves. They ate more than they provided, and it was only the male Pili who thought they had any value. Probably because the males were closer to the Korga in thought and action, she thought. There were enough troops left to protect the caves without the stupid beasts slavering about, and good riddance. Mayhaps they would not return. There was a pleasant thought.

Conan saw the approaching figures long before they arrived. His fiery blue eyes took in the scene, and he knew he was about to meet another batch of the Pili's dragonlike hounds. He rolled his shoulders, limbering them, and pulled his sword. A cursory glance told the

Cimmerian youth that there was no cover to be had. There was a small hill, not more than thrice his own height, a short ways to his left; that would give him the higher ground, something of an advantage, but not much. He had perhaps a minute or so before the reptilian creatures arrived, so he trotted toward the rise and began to climb.

When he was nearly to the top of the hillock, Conan almost fell into a pit. Due to the nature of the ground, he had not seen it until he was nearly upon it. The sandy depression was fairly deep, perhaps nearly his own height, and the sides were angled down sharply. Odd, the pit, he seemed to recall seeing something like it before, but he could not quite remember where.

Conan circumvented the pit and reached the pinnacle of the small hill. Perhaps one of the Korga would fall into the hole, were it moving fast enough to miss seeing it in time. True, it could climb out easily enough, but the effort would give Conan more time to dispatch the others.

He shifted his grip on the sword handle until it felt perfect. Seven of them. Bad odds. Well, if this were to be his last battle, he would sell himself as dearly as he could. He would arrive in front of Crom with as many of these beasts as he could bring. He hoped Crom had forgotten about their earlier meeting, but it had been recent enough that Conan doubted that happening.

The lizard beasts came, hissing and growling. They seemed to take no notice of the change in terrain, but clambered up the hillock in lunging bounds, teeth flashing in their scaled muzzles as they drew nearer.

Conan cocked the sword back over his right shoulder. Perhaps he could cleave through two at once, did he swing hard enough.

Perhaps some god felt benevolent this day, for the first of the onrushing beasts never thought to look for its footing and fairly sailed into the pit just below where Conan stood. The big Cimmerian, even though staring his death in the eyes, managed to find a smile. Foolish beast.

The other Korga, however, seeing the fate of their leader, slowed their headlong run and circled around the pit.

Conan shifted to his left as the sun's hot light flashed on the fangs of the nearest beast. As the thing lunged toward him, Conan swung the blued-iron blade with all his strength. The sword sang in the air as it bit into the Korga's neck, found a space between bones, and sheared the thing's head cleanly from its shoulders.

The headless body continued running, but past Conan.

Conan spun in time to meet the next Korga's charge. Continuing the motion of the blade, Conan opened the beast horizontally. Entrails spilled, and the lizard creature blinked and looked down, forgetting all about Conan.

But the other four were nearly upon him. Conan shifted his stance to recock the blade.

He could take one more, mayhaps two, were he lucky—

The first Korga screamed from the pit. It was a long cry that stopped as though sliced off by a razor.

Conan risked a glance toward the pit as another of the beasts impaled itself on his extended sword point.

Something was coming out of the pit, and it was not the Korga that had fallen into it.

In that instant, Conan recalled where he had seen the like before. It had been much, much smaller, and had belonged to a spidery creature that fed upon ants and other tiny insects unfortunate enough to slide into its trap.

What came from within this ground, however, was twice the size of the beasts, and it looked like a spider from the dream of a mad god. The monster was black and furry, eyeless, but with arm-thick mandibles that dripped smoking poison, and what seemed at least eight legs.

"Crom!"

Faster than he would have thought possible, the monster scrabbled up the hillock and attacked one of the surprised Korga. The click of the thing's mandibles was loud in the desert air; with one snap, it clipped the Korga in twain.

The remaining Korga scattered amidst loud and fearful hissings, and the monster turned toward the nearest and began to chase it. Big it was, and hideous, and faster than its scaled target.

Conan turned and sprinted in the opposite direction.

Perhaps the hellspawn preferred Pili dogs to human flesh, but Conan had no intention of finding out firsthand. Let it feast on the Korga until sated. And even as he ran, he resolved to watch more closely his own steps.

Kleg waded into the small lake, grinning. The rain continued, somewhat lighter now, but as the water rose up to his waist, then chest and neck, the rain ceased to matter.

He sank below the surface and began the Change.

With his first breath of water, gills sprouted along the sides of his neck. His bones stretched, sinews creaking as they followed, and his flesh began to shift. His legs elongated and at the same time fused into a single unit. His feet formed themselves into a tail, longer on the top than on the bottom. His arms drew in toward his sleek body, his hands flattening into fins. A dorsal fin sprouted from his back, a delta shape reaching upward, and other fins emerged from his ventral side. His eyes moved back, his mouth widened, and rows of serrated teeth pushed through the hardening gums.

In a few seconds, the Change was complete. What had been Kleg the manlike was now twice the length and covered with skin the texture of pumice, as deadly a thing that swam any salt sea.

With a flick of his tail, Kleg drove his metamorphosed form through the water. New senses told him that the thrashing scrat lay just ahead, waiting for its destiny.

And its destiny was . . . prey.

Around him in the water, Kleg was aware of his brothers also undergoing the Change, becoming as he was, seeking that which he sought, but Kleg was first, and he opened his massive jaws and bit deeply.

In a matter of moments, the clear blue water had turned a cloudy crimson, and the struggling scrat was no more.

EIGHT

Dimma floated through the halls of his castle toward the strong room that contained his most valuable treasures: the eight items that composed his recovery spell. Only one piece was lacking for completion, and soon his Prime selkie would return with that one piece.

Ah, to be solid again, never to fear that coldness and sudden shift into vaporous ether! Once he retained a body upon which he could depend, things would change in this realm. He would go forth in the flesh, sweeping all who stood before him aside, taking control of all he saw. He had practiced his spells for five hundred years, after all, and he would not make the same mistakes he had made before. He would be Dimma the Mist Mage no longer, but instead Dimma the Destroyer. Perhaps he would make himself king, and even allow Seg to be his queen—until he got bored with her, of course, and found some nubile beauty to replace her. And after that one, another and another. There was much to be done, after all the years of inactivity. Pleasures to be had, armies to be slain, villages and even countries to enslave, all at the whim of Dimma the Destroyer.

Yes. He much liked the sound of that.

Ahead, Conan saw the rocky outcrop that must be the habitat of the Pili. The three-toed tracks of the deceased Korga led directly toward the low stone mound, which seemed more a jumble of giant rocks piled upon the desert by a careless god than anything else.

Conan squatted and observed the mound. The Pili had chosen a location from which they could observe approach from any direction. Aside from occasional clumps of dry bush, the land was bare around the mound for half an hour's fast walk. Even using the sporadic cover of the bushes, it would take a skilled man to manage a surprise visit to the Pili. In daylight, a party of three or more would likely find it impossible, were even a half-blind guard posted.

There was the key, Conan decided. A careful man could sneak close under cover of night, assuming he kept downwind to avoid watch beasts. Assuming also that the Pili's night vision was no more sharp than a man's. Risky, perhaps, but was not Conan planning to be-

come a successful thief when he reached
Shadizar? One had to begin practice somewhere.

Conan moved to a roundish clump of brush
and settled into its shade. Darkness would not
be long in coming. He would wait; in the
meanwhile, he would sleep.

Kleg, his hunger sated and his form once
again that which resembled a man, looked up
at the clearing sky. The rain had finally diminished and, even as he watched, stopped en-
tirely. The late-afternoon air was cool and
evening fast approaching. They would resume
their homeward journey on the morrow, he
decided.

Awake in her bed, Thayla was restless. She
hoped her fool of a husband could recover the
talisman of the Tree Folk, but there was no
guarantee of success. That the Pili were in
decline could not be denied, but with that
magical token, they might establish themselves
far enough away from the trails of men to
become once again a powerful force. Then
those things that should be hers by right could
be made to happen, but until then, life might
be a precarious thing.

Thayla threw the silk sheet from her and lay
naked on the bed, her voluptuous body exposed
to the night air. She needed a male, she
decided, but she deemed none of those left
behind by her husband satisfactory. He had
taken the strongest and best ones with him,

and Thayla was certain he had done so deliberately to thwart her desires. As a married female, she was not allowed to lie with any other than her husband, but that was a formality as far as she was concerned. Still, the cream of the Pili had gone with the king, leaving behind mostly females, children, and old males, with a few young stalwarts who had strength, but little experience as lovers. She did not feel like teaching a new male old tricks on this night.

No, Thayla wanted a lover with power and grace and endurance and she wanted him now.

Too bad, she thought. Maybe a prayer to the Great Dragon will bring results, eh? A gift from the Gods?

The Queen of the Pili rolled over onto her stomach and clutched one of the silken pillows to her bosom. The Gods help those who help themselves, she thought, sighing. Which of the boring young males could she send her chambermaid to fetch?

Conan worked his way toward the rocky mound with the skill of a hunter stalking a wary deer. Under the blanket of night, even his sharp eyes had trouble seeing much detail in the desert, though the chore was made easier by the Pili themselves as he drew nearer.

A guttering, smoky torch mounted on the face of the stone revealed both a guard and the entrance to a cave.

Prone on the soft ground, Conan considered the scene.

The guard looked like a man at this distance, a bald man, wearing a kind of short, dark kilt and crossed straps over his chest. His skin seemed bluish in the dim light, though that was hard to tell for certain. A short, thin spear completed the Pili guard's costume, this weapon held in one hand, though it was more like a long arrow than a real spear. After searching for a bow, Conan spotted a wooden thrower lying on the ground next to the guard. He did not seem particularly alert, the guard, as he leaned against the wall behind him, appearing to be half-asleep.

The yawning entrance to the cave bothered Conan more than did the single guard. He had no love for such places, especially after his recent experience in a vast underground system full of giant worms, bloodbats, and other foul beasts. Still, he had come to rescue Hok, and if the boy was within, there was no help for it. It was not likely that the Pili would send him out should Conan ask.

The Cimmerian circled to his right, moving with great stealth, freezing at the smallest desert sound, until finally he was next to the rock wall to the guard's left. He moved closer, until he deemed it unlikely he could approach any more without being seen. During this time, the guard shifted from foot to foot once, slouched more against the wall, hawked and spat twice.

No, alertness did not seem one of this particular Pili's virtues.

Conan's plan was simple enough. He found a stone somewhat larger than his fist and gripped it in his right hand. With his left hand, he picked up a pebble, then tossed it past the guard. When the Pili turned to see what had made the noise, Conan would leap up and clout that bald head with the stone.

The pebble bounced from a flat patch of stone and skittered into the darkness.

The guard did not move, nor did he appear to take notice of the sound.

Well, probably the normal contractions of the mound under the cooling desert air made many such sounds each night and the guard was used to them. Conan should have thought of that.

He found a slightly larger pebble and tossed it.

The result was the same.

Perhaps the Pili were hard of hearing?

Conan picked up another stone, this one nearly as large as the rock he planned to use as a weapon. This would certainly get his attention. He heaved the rock.

The stone, easily the size of a small boy's fist, clattered past the guard's feet. Still the Pili did not react.

Conan stood and moved. If he had not heard that, neither would he hear Conan's footsteps.

Half a span away from the guard, Conan

lifted the rock to strike. He stepped closer. Then stopped.

The guard, leaning against the rock, was asleep on his feet. Conan raised his other hand and waved it in front of the guard's face. The Cimmerian grinned. Well. He would sleep more soundly in a moment. Conan lifted the rock.

Inside the cave, there were more torches set at irregular intervals along the corridor wall. Conan hurried along the corridor. The place had a musky smell that was not unpleasant, and the air was warmer than that outside. He was inside and that had been easy enough. Now all he had to do was find the boy and get back out.

No, Thayla decided, she would not awaken her chambermaid and have her fetch one of the young males. It would take more effort than it was worth. Instead, the queen arose from her bed and put on her wrap. Perhaps she would go for a walk in the night air. The Korga had not returned, so they would not hiss at her. That the animals had not come back disturbed Rawl the old one, but bothered Thayla not a whit. Stupid beasts.

She moved into the corridor outside her sleeping chamber—

Just in time to see a human pass by on the cross hall.

Thayla froze. He had not seen her, she was sure.

A man? Inside the caves? How?

Thayla started to raise the alarm, but stopped. Perhaps she was imagining things. Perhaps her desire had clouded her vision, and her mind was creating phantoms in the corridors. She smiled ruefully. Aye, it could be. And she could imagine her embarrassment if she roused the Pili only to be told they could not locate her dream.

Thayla walked toward the cross hall, stepped out into it, and looked for her dream man, expecting to see emptiness.

There he was. He rounded a turning as she watched, unaware of her.

She shook her head. She could smell that musky odor men had, could plainly see that impossibly broad and muscular body, could hear the shuffle of leather sandals on the stone floor. No, this was no dream, he was real! The largest one of his kind she had ever seen, wide shoulders and thick arms and legs and long, dark fur upon his head.

Thayla felt herself quivering. What was he doing here?

She began to follow him. It did not matter what he was doing here, she decided. The Gods had smiled upon her and granted her wish. Even if this were a dream, she meant to enjoy it to the fullest.

Conan felt a chill, and he stopped and looked around carefully. No one was apparent. Thus far, he had passed chambers in which sleeping Pili had lain, but he had not found Hok.

He moved deeper into the mound, searching.

Thayla went into a sleeping chamber and roused one of the young Pili males who had more muscle than brains.

"My queen!"

"Silence. Come with me."

The male obeyed.

Around a series of turnings Conan went. The entrance to a large chamber beckoned. He entered.

There against one wall stood a cage, and in it was the sleeping form of the boy Hok.

Conan moved toward the cage. Finally.

The door to the cage was bolted shut with a complex series of levers that could not be reached from within, but which Conan could work easily enough from without. He moved toward the throw lever. Best not to wake the boy yet, he decided, lest he cry out in surprise.

"Stand there," Thayla ordered the young male. "Here, take this." She handed him a long, wrist-thick pole normally used to knock nesting bats from the ceiling.

Then the Queen of the Pili moved to stand in the entrance to the jail chamber.

"Ho, man," she said.

At the sound of a soft voice, Conan spun and drew his sword.

Standing in the dim corridor's light was a

woman. She was bald and wearing some flimsy wrap. Even as he watched, she shrugged the covering off. The wrap formed a pool around her feet and she stood there naked.

Conan stared. Bald she might be, but she did not lack any of the usual curves of a woman. Her breasts were heavy and full, her hips wide and promising, her arms outstretched as if in invitation. She might be a Pili, but she was no less comely for that. Conan had seen few women who had more to offer than did this one.

The woman—no, the Pili—smiled at him.

"Come," she said. "I have something for you." She ran one hand down her hip, then back up to touch her breast.

Well, he was not so foolish as to dally with a woman in the midst of an enemy camp, but he had best ensure her silence. Conan moved quickly to catch the woman as she turned and began to walk out of his sight.

She was only two spans distant when he entered the corridor, moving directly away from him, and he was taken with the lush shape of her back and buttocks and legs—

And then the world suddenly flashed red with pain and dwindled to black around him.

NINE

The selkies were nearly ready to leave when the rear guard came running into the camp. "Prime! The lizard men come!"

Kleg grabbed the panting selkie by the shoulders. "What foolishness is this?"

The selkie managed to catch his breath. "An army of them, Prime, thousands!"

"Idiot! The Pili do not number in the thousands!"

"Hundreds, then."

"Somebody put a spear through this babbling fool."

"Dozens, Prime, I swear on my birth egg!"

"Show me."

A quick ascent of one of the nearby hills and Kleg stood next to the scout looking into the distance.

Well, by the balls of He Who Creates, the

scout was right. There had to be at least seven or eight dozen of the lizard men, along with those toothed reptiles they used as hunting beasts, marching directly along the trail the selkies had traveled a day earlier. What were they up to, these Pili? This was certainly a war party, and there were no settlements between the Pili and the village of Karatas on the lip of the Home Lake. True, the lizard men could be going to try and sack Karatas, but that was unlikely, the village being surrounded on three sides by a tall and well-defended palisade, with the Sargasso at its back. No, these lizard men likely had something else in mind, and Kleg had a premonition that he knew what it was: his own party. Such a thing did not bode well for the much smaller group of selkies. But why? They had nothing the lizard men could possibly want, nothing of value. . . .

Kleg slapped his head with the heel of his hand in sudden realization: the talisman! And how had they found out about it? Why, Kleg, Prime servant of He Who Creates, supposedly the most clever of the selkies, had practically *told* them—he had given them that blasted man child, who had no doubt talked before he was consumed. The boy had seen Kleg take the damned thing. Blast!

Kleg turned and scurried down the hill, the scout behind him. The lizard men were no faster on land than were the selkies. They were at least an hour behind, and if they left immediately, Kleg and his troop could maintain that lead all the way to the Sargasso. Once there, the denizens of the weed would halt any pursuit; any that managed to straggle through would face the wrath of He Who Creates, an unpleasant prospect at best and certainly a fatal one.

If, however, the lizard men should somehow gain an hour, the odds were too long in their favor. And Kleg *had* to return home with the talisman.

He decided what needed to be done. He called his troop to gather around him. There were only a dozen left after the diversion at the trees, but they should prove sufficient if correctly utilized.

"We are pursued by the lizard men," Kleg said. "They outnumber us perhaps eight to one. We cannot fail in our mission, so I shall go ahead and leave you to slow them."

This produced a not unexpected reaction from the selkies, a grumbling response common to every soldier who had ever lived.

"But wait," Kleg said. "There is a river half a day ahead of us, one no doubt made much deeper by the storms of yesterday. We will journey there, and you shall all Change and wait for them in the water."

The group brightened somewhat at this order. Selkies had certain basic skills on land, but in the water, no lizard man would be a match for one. Dispatching half a dozen or more each ought not to be a problem, they would be thinking, and Kleg sweetened the order by saying, "Once you have slaughtered the lizards, you may return home, and I am certain I can convince He Who Creates to reward each of you with at least two new wives and access to the best feeding grounds."

A ragged cheer went up from the selkies. The way to a selkie's heart was through his stomach, and if that entry was not enough, well, the other route would usually suffice. Both together could not be denied. Food and females, Kleg thought, it worked every time.

"Come let us depart and make ready for our enemies."

Conan awoke, swimming up through murky depths to find that he did not recall where he was or how he had come to be there; more, his head hurt exceedingly. Had he drank too much wine?

The Cimmerian sat up, and saw that he was in a cage. Next to him was the boy Hok.

Ah. Now he remembered. There had been a beautiful bald woman, naked, beckoning him. That was the last thing he recalled before the sky fell on him.

"Ah, my stalwart man is awake at last," came a voice.

Conan turned. It was her, the woman. No, not a woman, a Pili, though for purposes of looks, there seemed little difference, save for the lack of hair and the blue tint to her skin. She wore a red wrap he had last seen bunched at her feet.

More torches had been set aflame, so that the interior of the cave was quite bright, and when the Pili woman saw Conan look at her, she moved her hands slightly and the wrap gaped wide down her front, revealing again the bare breasts and other delights he had noticed before.

"I see you find me somewhat attractive," she said.

Indeed, Conan thought, she could not help but notice that. He shifted his position slightly.

The Pili woman laughed. When she moved closer, Conan could see that her eyes were catlike, the pupils narrow and diamond-shaped. And her face was not ugly, though he spent little time looking at that portion of her, since her slow walk caused other parts of her to move in a much more interesting manner than her face.

Though the squarish pattern of the cage's bars would allow Conan to reach through them, the Pili woman stopped well out of his grasp. "I am Thayla, Queen of the Pili," she said. "Welcome to our caves."

"You always keep your guests in cages?"

"Usually. But fear not, you shall be released soon. How may I address you, my stalwart man?"

"I am Conan, of Cimmeria."

"Are all the men of your Cimmeria so ... large?" She waved at him, and for a moment, Conan thought there was more to her comment than it seemed. He must be mistaken.

"Nay."

"Then I must consider myself especially blessed to be able to take you in," she said. "Why have you come here?"

"To fetch the boy." He nodded at Hok. "The selkies stole him."

"Ah. Well, perhaps some bargain might be arranged."

"I have nothing of value save my sword," Conan said.

She smiled. "Indeed. It seems a mighty weapon."

Conan looked at where his sword lay, on the floor behind the queen, but she was looking at him.

What, he wondered, did the queen wish of him? He knew that the Pili ate his kind, but the hunger in her eyes seemed to him of a different kind than one lusting for food.

The waterway that had been little more than a meandering stream when the selkies crossed it outbound now raged past, a churning brown river of mud and foam, carrying sticks and other detritus along at a heady speed. Even Changed, the selkies would be hard-pressed to maintain their position against such a current. The timing on this would be tricky, Kleg realized.

The leader of the selkies dispatched a scout to watch for the arrival of the lizard men. He would have his troops wait until the last moment before entering the turbulent waters for their attack.

Kleg himself waded into the river, feeling the powerful tug of the current at his legs. He dropped the water's embrace, shifted his form as quickly as he could, and swam across to the opposite bank. It was a difficult task, as powerful as he was. When he attained the far shore, he had been carried hundreds of spans downriver.

After resuming his upright form, Kleg walked back to the river's narrowest width, the place the lizards would logically make their crossing. Being land dwellers and poor swimmers, the pursuers would likely attempt to build some kind of ferry. A line strung across the river by some bravo would be followed by a thicker rope, and a raft constructed to be worked along the rope. There were plenty of trees about, but even so, the raft would take several hours to build, at least, and that in itself should buy Kleg enough time to be safely away and far ahead of the lizards. When the raft was overturned and at least some of the lizards turned into carrion, it would take more time to catch the raft or perhaps even to build another. Kleg figured he could count on at least half a day gained thusly, perhaps more.

The Prime selkie grinned. He waved at his troops, motioning for them to move upriver, to allow for the current. They would hide there in the thick brush and wait for the lizards; once the raft was constructed, they would slip into the water and attack. It was a good plan, Kleg felt.

Being the author of such a tactic pleased Kleg,

and he felt it only right that he stay and watch it put into practice. An hour more would make little difference, since he would gain a dozen times that; what survivors remained would never catch him with that kind of lead, assuming they even bothered to continue.

So Kleg found a comfortable spot and awaited the upcoming slaughter with a certain amount of gleeful anticipation.

The queen left Conan in the cage, alone with Hok.

"They are going to *eat* us!" Hok said.

"Perhaps not," Conan said. "The queen has indicated that some accommodation might be reached."

"She lies. She said I would go free if I told her what the fishmen wanted at our grove. I said, but she only laughed at me when I asked her to open the cage."

Conan nodded. So, the queen was not to be trusted. Good to know.

"We aren't eaten yet, boy," he said. "We shall see what happens." He brushed several small rocks to one side, clearing a space on the floor, then stretched out flat.

"What are you doing?" Hok asked.

"Going to sleep."

"How can you sleep? We must find a way out!"

"The way out is through the door, boy. When they come and open it, then we shall have a way out. In the meanwhile, I am tired, so I shall sleep."

"But—but—but—"

"Awaken me if they begin to eat us."

With that, Conan closed his eyes and drifted into slumber, albeit a light one. The boy was fretful and rightfully so, but there was nothing to be done at the moment and Conan might need his strength later. He felt certain that the Queen of the Pili was not quite ready to make soup of him just yet. She had something else in mind.

Three chambermaids scurried around in her sleeping quarters, cleaning the queen's room.

"Fresh pillows!" Thayla ordered. "Make them thick ones. And burn incense, the pungent black kind. Hurry!"

As Thayla watched her maids rush to freshen her chamber, she felt an excited flutter in her belly. Such a giant of a man would doubtless furnish her with much pleasure! She could hardly wait. She might keep him for days before her husband returned. They could have the boy for the festival, but this large man would not be consumed until she had worn him to exhaustion. However long it took.

She much looked forward to the task.

Things were not going according to Kleg's plan.

First, the lizard men had not bothered to send a line across the river with a swimmer.

Well, all right, that was no great problem. If they built enough rafts to carry all their troops, or didn't mind following the raft downstream to return it for another crossing, so much the better. That would take even more time.

But instead of starting to fell trees, the lizards had begun to unpack things from several large containers they carried. Tents, perhaps? Were they planning on being here long enough to require a camp?

From his hidden vantage point across the wide river, Kleg smiled. Even better. He was practically home free—

Wait. What were they doing now?

A dozen of the lizards scurried about, each carrying what looked like bellows. What . . . ?

As Kleg watched, the lizards began pumping air into the tents—no, not tents, but some kind of large skin bags. These were sewn in such a way that they inflated easily, forming oblong if somewhat squashed-looking eggs. . . .

Floats. They weren't going to make a raft, they planned to cross the river on these skin bags!

Kleg's moment of panic quickly passed. Well, so they had floats; it mattered not. So much the better. His selkies would have less problems with these than with a wooden raft. One pass, one bite, and the floats would pop like foam bubbles!

Kleg had to see this. It would be a slaughter, truly.

It was but a matter of minutes before a

dozen of the floats were fully inflated and made ready. Eight or nine lizards gathered around each float and hustled it to the water's edge. Kleg's anticipation grew. Ah, to be in the water and enjoying the feast himself!

But the lizards did not launch the floats as expected. Instead, one of them passed along the line of troops, carrying a large earthen pot. The lizards began to dip the tips of their throwing darts into the pot. Some kind of ritual?

Kleg's eyes widened as he realized what was happening.

The short spears came out of the pot with their tips a smoldering red that glistened in the daylight.

Poison!

The lizards started their crossing, and while three or four of them on each float wielded paddles, the other four or five stood with their dart slingers held high, watching the water!

Kleg stared. Upstream, the scout would have given the word to the dozen selkies, who by now would be in the river and moving to attack. The angle of a Changed selkie's jaws would require that they roll onto their backs to bite the floats, exposing their bellies! The floats rode high in the water, so the selkies would be close to the surface when they came for the floats.

Kleg knew he should run, should gain as much time as possible, but he was frozen in place, watching.

The first float into the water began to drift

rapidly downstream as it gained a little in the crossing. The lizards began to hurl their poisoned spears, yelling as they did so.

The float deflated suddenly and the lizards screamed as they fell into the water, but Kleg recognized the thrashing forms of three of his dozen selkies in their death throes, spears sticking out of their poison-maddened bodies.

More floats began the crossing. More darts were thrown. Some of the lizards went down as their floats were deflated, but most did not.

Kleg managed to find his feet. At least a third of the lizards would finish the crossing, and all or nearly all of his selkies would sleep with the fishes when it was over.

Kleg had miscalculated. They were only minutes behind him now.

He ran for his life.

TEN

Conan awoke feeling somewhat refreshed, to find the boy Hok staring nervously at him. He sought to put the boy at ease.

"Fear not," Conan said. "I have a plan."

Hok's eyes widened. "Really?"

"Aye. When the lizard men come for us, they will open the door and we shall pretend to be docile. Once out, I shall overcome them and thus we shall make good our escape."

The boy stared. His mouth gaped. "*That* is your plan?"

"Simple, is it not?"

"Simple-minded, more like."

"I am open to other suggestions," Conan said, feeling somewhat irritated at Hok.

"Why do we not turn into birds and fly away? Or maybe squirrels? That is as likely to happen as your plan."

"For such a small boy you seem to be burdened with more than your share of tongue, Hok."

"For such a large man, your wit seems rather small—"

"Shhh. Someone comes."

Hok stilled his voice at the sound of approaching footsteps on the stone floor.

It was the queen, and she was alone.

"I have come to invite you to my chamber, Conan my stalwart."

"Gladly I accept," Conan said. "If you would but open the door."

"Oh, to be sure, I shall open it wide for you," she said.

Conan did not have to fake his smile. This was going to be almost too easy.

The Queen of the Pili raised her right hand, closed into a loose fist. "But first a small guarantee of your cooperation." With that, she opened her hand and flung into Conan's face some kind of powder.

Before he could stop himself, Conan sucked in a quick breath. He sneezed and tried to cough the powder from his lungs, but it was too late. As his consciousness faded, taken from him by the dust the queen had thrown, Conan had time for a final thought:

Perhaps he was going to have a harder time of this than he had thought.

When next Conan awoke, he found himself lying on silken cushions next to the Queen of

Pili. He, like she, was altogether naked. And he was feeling rather tired.

The queen smiled at him. "Ah, my stalwart man arises yet again."

Conan stared at her. His thoughts were muddled. She had drugged him, he recalled. And she must have had him taken to her chambers.

"You have been magnificent," she said, touched his shoulder with her fingertips. "None has ever done better."

"I have done nothing," Conan managed.

"You are too modest. Surely you recall?"

"I recall you flinging a powder into my face."

"And nothing since? Ah, if that was how you behaved when asleep, I cannot help but wonder how much better you shall do when awake!"

Conan shook his head, trying to clear it. What was she talking about?

The queen then rolled toward him, and showed him exactly what she meant.

Kleg called for the curses of ten thousand gods to fall upon the lizard men, but he had no intention of stopping to see if the imprecation worked. At first he thought to hide, that surely a single selkie would be more difficult to find than a dozen, but given the unknown tracking abilities of the lizards, he decided not to chance it. No, speed would be his best ally. One selkie could certainly move as fast as a troop of lizards, especially given that the lizards sought only booty, while the selkie ran for his skin.

Kleg wove his way through the thick forest

as the day wore down to night, and while he saved his breath for his physical efforts, his mind continued to conjure up curses against his chasers.

Conan arose from the queen's bed, not a little tired himself, and found his clothes. The effects of the drug had long since worn off, but the queen finally slept.

He found his sword under a cushion that had been thrown across the room earlier. Likely there were guards posted without, but obviously they had been instructed not to enter the chamber unless specifically called upon to do so; had mere noise been the signal, they would have burst in on Conan and the queen half a dozen times already.

Conan grinned. He could not say that his visit with the lizard woman had been unpleasant; indeed, he found it most difficult to think of her as other than a human woman, given her actions thus far.

Conan stuck his head through the chamber's opening. There were two guards, one on either side of the door. Softly, the Cimmerian said, "Hark, the queen wishes to convey a message." His voice was little more than a confidential whisper.

The two guards looked at each other, then back at Conan.

Conan waved them closer, grinning like a conspirator.

The two grinned, doubtless thinking themselves men of the world, and leaned toward Conan.

The Cimmerian grabbed each guard by the neck and slammed their heads together, hard. There came a sound like a gourd dropped on stone. When he released the guards, they fell like poleaxed oxen.

Conan hurried down the hallway to fetch Hok.

When Thayla awoke, she did so smiling. Who would have thought . . . ?

Where was he?

She sat up abruptly. Conan was gone! How had he gotten out?

"Guards! To me!"

Nothing happened. Thayla leaped up and ran to the doorway.

The two guards lay sprawled on the cavern floor unconscious.

By the Great Dragon!

"To arms!" Thayla screamed. She had to find him, and quickly. It would not do to have a human running around who might speak of his actions with the Queen of the Pili, especially when such speech might reach the wrong ears.

Her husband's ears.

"To arms!"

Conan ran across the desert to the east, the boy Hok next to him.

"But how did you escape?" Hok asked. "Did you smite the queen with your sword?"

"Save your breath for running, boy."

"It takes no breath to listen."

"Ask your sister when you see her. Better still, ask your brother, Tair."

If he continued moving through the night, Kleg would reach the village of Karatas on the Home Lake early the next day. Once there, he would be safe, for although the village was peopled largely by humans, there were also others of his own kind here and there, and all paid obeisance to He Who Creates. Once he reached the Sargasso, he could Change and wend his way through the weed paths to the underwater castle entrance, the talisman held safely in his teeth. There were creatures in the weed who would challenge even a Changed selkie, but not many, and none who could catch one in open water. Yes. A few more hours and he would be in the clear.

As darkness painted the earth with her colors of gray and black, Kleg ran, calling on all his strength and speed. He could rest when he got home; to tarry now would mean death.

When it was determined that Conan and the human boy were nowhere to be found inside the caves, Thayla assembled a dozen of the remaining males into a tracking force.

"We must find the escaped man and boy," she said. "It is most important."

Some of the males snickered at this, but Thayla cut their laughter short with a baleful stare. "Should they *not* be caught, I shall explain to the king that you allowed them to escape."

The dozen young males became serious. She knew what they would be thinking: whatever else happened, she *was* the queen, and she had the king firmly gripped where a male was most sensitive. If it came to it, whom was he more likely to believe?

Very serious indeed.

"I shall lead this expedition myself," she said. Thayla allowed a moment for this to sink in, a female leading males, but if there were any objections, no one voiced them. She could not trust them to return and tell her that Conan had been slain; she had to see it for herself.

"Let us depart, then," the Queen of the Pili said.

And depart they did.

Deep in his strong room, Dimma had a sudden premonition. His Prime servant was somehow in danger.

Dimma willed himself toward the door. He could move slowly in this fashion, though even a stray breeze could divert him. He felt that if Kleg were dead, he would know it, and it did not seem that such was the case; still, if Kleg had obtained the prize he sought, he must return with it. To that end, Dimma could send other of his thralls to ensure that if Kleg had collected the magic Seed, he would be certain to finish the remainder of his journey, albeit he might not be alive to do it. The life of one selkie meant nothing, even if the selkie did happen to be the Prime. There were always others who could be elevated to that position.

All who served Dimma knew the penalty for failure and it would not do to allow any to forget it, even for an instant. One could not have too many examples made to remind all of such things. If Kleg had *failed*, whatever remained of his corpse would be hung where all could see. If he accomplished his labor, then he would be sent to the deep with honor, his reputation secure. What else could he wish for other than the thanks of his god?

ELEVEN

Conan and Hok had not run far when they noticed pursuit. Conan made to draw his sword, then stopped.

"Hold here," the Cimmerian said.

A party of about ten figures came toward them, and as they drew nearer, Hok's face broke into a wide smile.

"Cheen!"

Indeed, as Conan had seen, the followers were of the Tree Folk.

A few moments later, the group arrived. Cheen hugged her brother, and there were smiles all around.

Cheen clasped Conan tightly. "Thank you, Conan, for saving my brother!"

Despite his recent encounter with the lizard queen, Conan felt himself warm to Cheen's embrace. Conan's own arms seemed to surround the woman unbidden by thought.

Cheen moved from Conan's embrace to look up into his face. "We were trying to devise a way into the Pili's mound when we saw you and Hok flee. How did you manage it?"

"The queen took him away," the boy said before Conan could speak. "He won't tell me how he did it, but they were gone a long time and—"

"I shall explain it all later," Conan interrupted hastily. "Now it would be best if we departed."

Cheen gave him a doubtful look, then finally nodded. "Aye. Tair and the rest continued following the selkies' trail. They'll want our help."

"And the lizard men might field pursuit," Conan said.

"We have achieved half our goal," Cheen said. She ruffled Hok's hair. "I am glad to see you, little brother."

They started off.

Kleg continued moving through the night and it was well that he did so, for he was never more than half an hour in front of his pursuers. He could not be certain that they even knew he existed, but a search of the dead selkies would not have revealed the talisman; doubtless the lizard men continued to follow, still seeking that same item.

Came the glimmerings of dawn and Kleg's step faltered somewhat; despite his great strength, his flight had tired him more than a little. His goal lay near at hand, though. The stark palisade of the village of Karatas rose to meet the morning's mists just ahead.

To the east of the settlement stood what appeared to be a rocky hill. Upon closer examination, the hill proved to be a single, huge chunk of rock, all of a piece, and the rays of the sleepy sun revealed this eminent boulder's single hue to be a deep and rich jet. Against the greenery of trees and grass, the black rock stood out like a blotch of dark paint on an albino's pale arm. The village, Kleg knew, had been named after this geologic phenomenon, for the name Karatas itself meant "black rock" in the tongue of those who had first settled the area.

Kleg hurried toward the towering wall of wood ahead of him. The magic talisman bumped his waist within the pouch he wore. Nearly safe, he was. True, one could enter the crater lake anywhere and make one's way through the Sargasso, but the unexplored weed was fraught with dangers. The safest tunnels through the growth began where the village met the water; besides, once inside the city, the lizard men's pursuit would end. The gates might be opened for a single Pili, but certainly not for an armed force of them; the administrators of Karatas wanted no more trouble than already existed within the protective walls. The Pili would know as much.

The wall loomed. Kleg came to stand under

the guard post mounted over the smaller of the two gates on the road leading to the village.

"Ho, the gate watch!"

A fat, bearded man helmeted in a bowllike morion leaned out to look down at Kleg. "Aye, 'tis the watch. Who calls?"

"Kleg, Prime servant of He Who Creates, seeking entrance."

The guard moved back from sight, and the long bronze lever that controlled the smaller door creaked in its channel. An instant later, the iron-backed door swung outward on its thick, oiled hinges. "Enter, Prime."

Kleg smiled as he strode into the village. They knew him here, and they wanted no trouble with his master, upon whose sufferance they existed. He Who Creates could, if He so desired, magically wipe the village away as easily as a selkie crushing a water bug, and all who resided therein surely must know it.

When the gate swung shut behind him, Kleg felt a sense of relief. He would find a place to eat and to rest before going into the Sargasso. He could afford to spend a day recuperating, now that the end of his quest had drawn so near.

There was an oasis in the desert across which Conan, Cheen, and the others trekked, a splash of greenery that edged a spring-fed pond, and it was to this oasis that the group made their way under the oppressive heat of the sun.

As the men and women of the Tree Folk's

party filled their water skins and rested in the cool shade, Cheen took Conan aside.

"Much as I would like to continue, we should rest and wait here until evening," she said. "The desert drinks the life of those who seek to cross this part of it on foot during the day."

Conan nodded. There had been no sign of pursuit from the Pili, and desert travel was best done under the cool moon and not her hotter brother, the sun.

"Come and explain what Hok spoke of, regarding the Queen of the Pili," Cheen said, laying her hand on Conan's arm. "There is a quiet place, just over there, beneath the shade of that flowered bush, where we will not be disturbed."

Conan looked at the swelling of Cheen's breasts under the thin shirt she wore, at the tightness of her muscles, and at the bright smile she gave him. He became aware that it was very possible his explanation would be accompanied by a demonstration, and despite his resolve about women, at the moment the idea was not unpleasant in the least.

"Aye," he said, returning her smile.

Thayla's tracker found the place where Conan and the boy had been joined by others, so that their party now matched the queen's own number. The Pili set off to follow, but shortly thereafter, a desert wind began to blow, stirring the sand and dust, and within minutes, the tracks of the escapees and their new companions were completely obscured.

Thayla led her troop across the desert, a mixture of fear and anger simmering in her hot blood. How dare that man leave before she was done with him? And what would happen to her if ever her husband should stumble onto Conan?

One of her troopers made to approach the queen. "Should we not go to the oasis, milady?"

The queen shook her head. "We are Pili, we can travel without water."

"Beg your pardon, milady, that is true, *we* can, but the humans might—"

"We will pass the oasis," she said, "and perhaps in so doing get ahead of them, where we can set a trap."

"Ah," the trooper said. "Wise."

Thayla did not bother to reply to his flattery. Were she wise, they would be feasting on cooked manflesh in the mound and not chasing their dinner across the desert.

From the castle that rode the Sargasso, Dimma sent forth a magical call. There responded to the command a number of unnatural beings who owed their existence to earlier magicks of the Mist Mage: skreeches arose from the lake's depths, joined by the eels of power, and finally, the gigantic and omnivorous Kralix.

The skreeches were half-fish and half something that resembled women, and in the air, their voices in concert produced a hypnotic drone that drew those who heard as spilled honey draws flies. A man unwary enough to fall into the clutches of a skreech would find himself dead in short order, for the skreeches drank blood. A dozen of them swam up to answer their master's call.

The eels of power attained at full growth the length of a tall man and the thickness of his arm, and each bore within its body an energy akin to the lightning from a storm. To touch an eel in the water was to die stunned and blasted. A score of the eels came to the summons.

The Kralix was one of a kind. It was twice the size of an ox, its skin a glistening, mottled gray green, and it would eat plant or flesh with equal interest, and could swim the waters or stalk the land with nearly equal ability. It most resembled a thing that might have been born of wolf, bear, and toad, had the three somehow mated together, and its curse was that it felt neither pain nor joy. All the Kralix ever felt was hunger, and unleashed, it would eat itself into a stupor. It was an amphibian nightmare, the Kralix, and its power was unequaled by any beast in the lake and few that had ever walked the land.

Dimma sent these minions into the weed, toward the village that perched on the rim of the water. "Go," he said. "Go and find my Prime selkie and escort him to me."

Obediently, they went.

Dimma floated in his throne room. The skreeches and eels would be limited to the lake,

but the Kralix could attain the land. Certainly
its appearance in the village would be cause for
consternation. Dimma smiled at the thought.
Given enough time, the Kralix could chew its
way through the palisade wall itself, and Dimma
had given it the essence of his Prime selkie as a
guide. Wherever Kleg was, the Kralix would
find him. And woe be to anybody or anything
that got in the Ranafrosch's path. . . .

Under the thick bush in the oasis, Conan
leaned on one elbow, grinning at Cheen. As he
had hoped, his explanation of his adventures
with the lizard queen had ended in a demonstration of sorts. Cheen's responses had been
most enthusiastic.

Cheen returned his smile. "I had wondered
about you since we met," she said.

"And now?"

"Now my curiosity is well satisfied."

Now that he had recovered Hok, Conan wondered about the second part of their quest.
"What of the magic talisman?"

Cheen sat up and began to dress. Conan felt a
slight stab of regret, for she was very comely
without her clothes. He decided that he much
liked women with a certain amount of muscle.
It was both attractive and useful.

"I am attuned to the Seed," Cheen said.
"Wherever it might be, if I can but get close
enough, it will call to me."

That should make things somewhat easier,
Conan decided. He said as much.

Cheen finished dressing. "We should rest," she said. "We leave when the sun begins his sleep."

Conan nodded. He lay back on the cushion of dead leaves and soft earth and, within moments, fell into a deep slumber untroubled by dreams.

Kleg sat alone in one corner of a small and uncrowded inn called, for reasons no one seemed to remember, the Wooden Fish. The innkeeper, a bald, stout, pockmarked man of advanced years, set before the selkie a platterful of cooked eel and raw mussels, as well as a tankard of kral, a potent and aromatic beverage favored by Kleg's kind. He had heard men refer to kral as smelling like a night chamber and tasting like pond scum, but to a selkie, the beverage was sweet and fresh, and far better than the vinegary wines men drank.

Kleg felt much better than he had for several days. He had food, drink, and a room for the day. He would eat and drink, sleep while the sands of the day ran down to night, then arise and look up a few old friends in the evening cool, waiting until dawn again to begin the final leg of his journey. He deserved the rest, he knew, and a single day more would mean little against the vast scale of time, given that he had accomplished his mission. He Who Creates might grumble at Kleg's slowness, but such noises would be lost in the joy of the prize. Moreover, He Who Creates would certainly not wish for the talisman to be lost during the swim due to tiredness on the part of its bearer. Of that, Kleg had no doubt he could convince his master.

The selkie chewed thoughtfully on a section of eel. It was badly cooked, the eel, and spiced worse, but that was a small matter. In another few days, Kleg would be free to roam the Sargasso, and would dine on fresher fare seasoned in its own hot blood. The thought of it brought a smile to Kleg's face, and his white teeth gleamed brightly in the flickering light of the tapers.

TWELVE

Thayla's plan to circle well past the oasis and set a trap for the escapees and their new band seemed to her without flaw. The Queen of the Pili had high hopes that the encounter would be brief and bloody, ending with more meat for the table than her kind had seen in many moons. From disaster could come triumph. When her foolish husband returned, the evidence of her impropriety would be steaming in the kettle, or perhaps slowly roasting over a low fire. Indeed, with as much food as the ambushed party represented, she would have a triumph she could lord over her husband for a long, long time, especially should he fail to obtain the forest talisman.

The shortest and most reasonable path to the east from this part of the desert required a traveler to pass among a series of shifting

dunes not more than a few moments' walk
ahead of Thayla and her band. These mounds
of fine, powdery sand stood at their tallest
more than a dozen times the height of a Pili,
and their contours shifted from month to month,
sometimes even from day to day. The winds
shaped the sands, moving the drifts slowly but
surely, so that where they lay upon the desert
now was a far remove from where they had
been even twenty winters past. Smooth valleys
tended to form between the towering dunes,
and these valleys became natural pathways.

When they reached the dunes, Thayla followed the widest entry path for a short distance. "Here," she said. She divided her force
and ordered it into position.

"You, you, and you, climb that hillock and
hide behind the crest. You and you, ascend yon
sandy rock. The four of you, over there. You
and you and *you*, with me, over here."

The dozen Pili were thus arranged so that
when the escapees entered the valley, they
would be surrounded.

"Oh, and a special reward for the one whose
spear slays the large man, the one who fled our
hospitality."

That remark would ensure that virtually all
the troops would concentrate on Conan. To be
even more certain, Thayla added, "And should
he escape again, I will have all of your hides
for a carpet to floor the Korga pens."

The attack from higher ground would give
her troops the advantage, Thayla felt, and even

if the slaughter was not complete, Conan would certainly die. That was, after all, the important thing.

As the sun settled low to begin his nightly rest, Thayla climbed the squeaky sands, to wait.

Conan and the small group of Tree Folk moved across the dark desert, water bottles full, enjoying the coolness of the night. Under the moon's pale gaze, a series of humps arose from the flat desert ahead of them.

"The dunes," Cheen said. "That means the end of the desert is not far. We will be well clear by first light."

Conan regarded the dunes. He felt a chill colder than the night air warranted prickle his spine. "I like this not," he said.

Cheen looked at the Cimmerian. "I do not take your meaning."

"Travel in the dark is made bearable by the ability to see for such a long distance." He waved one arm to indicate the flat bareness of the desert around them. "In those hills of sand, our view will be much impeded."

"So?"

"So, we have seen no sign of pursuit by the Pili."

"We should thank the Green Goddess for such good fortune. Perhaps they chose not to follow."

"Aye. But the Queen of the Pili did not strike

me as someone who would allow us to escape unmolested."

"Does this worry of yours reach some conclusion?"

Conan shrugged. "The Pili would know that we could see them coming for a long way on the desert, giving us time to prepare a defense. But in those hills ahead, they might hide until we came very close. We could be trapped."

"You worry needlessly. It is unlikely the dunes hold hidden Pili."

"Unlikely, perhaps. Not impossible."

"What would you have us do?"

"Go around."

"That is not a good idea. Going around would cost us hours; we would be caught in the desert sun for at least another half day, perhaps longer."

Conan shook his head. Why did it seem as if he had spent the greater part of his life of late arguing with women? They must like it, he thought, for no more reason than the sake of the argument itself. Surely it was better to cook under a desert sun for half a day than to leave one's bones bleaching on the sands for eternity? But he did not say so aloud; instead, he loosened his sword in its scabbard and vowed to approach the passage ahead with special caution, no matter what Cheen said.

The single man standing night watch at the main gate of Karatas was bored. He could hardly be blamed for being so; after all, the last real threat to the city from without had come in the time of his father's father. The village was somewhat under the protection of the Mist Mage, at least enough so that any of the roving bands of bandits who might not be deterred by the palisade were loath to try Dimma's power. The region was remote enough so that no king with a great army and a wizard of his own cared to bother with a small village on the edge of a big lake with few riches to offer. True, the guard thought—and the dullness of his watch offered much time for thinking, though he was not overburdened with an apparatus for cerebration—there were a few attractive women, some passable wines, and even a little gold here. Hardly enough of all three together to be considered sufficient booty by a king with an army to feed and clothe, however.

Having entertained this particular train of thinking more than a few times during the boring seasons of his watch, the guard could not be bothered to worry when, from his perch on the wall, he saw a single Pili approaching the village in the silvery moonlight. The guard's beard was shot full of gray and he had been assigned this watch since before that beard had begun to fully sprout. The most dangerous incident he had faced in all that time had been a drunken farmer who threw rotten melons at him. And missed.

The guard had seen lizard men before. They were rare in these parts, to be sure, but probably half a dozen had passed through the gates during his watch at one time or another, so the guard was not one to gape at the sight of a Pili, even one with a decidedly regal bearing such as this one had.

"Alert, the watch!" the Pili called.

"Alert, indeed," the guard called back. "What be your business here?"

"I carry a message for one of the fishmen. Permit me to enter."

Even though the lizard man carried a long spear, the guard felt no particular peril. He tugged at the lever that opened the smaller entrance. Below him, the door began to swing open.

The Pili turned and shouted something into the darkness in a tongue the guard did not understand.

"What ... ?" the guard began. He stopped when he caught sight of at least a score of spear-carrying lizard men running toward the gate. "Hey!"

The guard tried to reverse the lever. The greenish bronze suddenly seemed slippery in his hands. This was bad business!

"Here!" came a voice.

The guard looked, and saw the first Pili standing below him, inside the gate, The guard was still deciding whether to question, threaten, or plead with the lizard man when the thrown spear struck him solidly in the center of the chest. He was filled with hot pain, but only for an instant. The pain stopped, he became numb, then he could not feel anything.

The guard's final thought was an odd one. After all the years of dullness, something exciting had finally happened.

Kleg awakened after the cloak of night had fallen over the village. He felt much better. He arose, drenched himself with the bowl of wash water in the room, and thus refreshed, left the room on the inn's third and highest floor, intending to eat another meal before going out.

As the selkie reached the stair landing, he chanced to glance out through the small window cut through the outer wall. The sky's cloth of darkness was pierced by the sharp pinpricks of uncountable stars and easily half the grinning moon, and a cool breeze carried the living odor of the lake through the opening. Kleg felt quite good, until he happened to look down through the window.

There on the narrow street between the inn and the leather shop across it, several figures scurried along. Between the moon's glow and that of a fat-fueled torch mounted on the side of the inn at street level, it was easy for the selkie's sharp eyes to tell that the trotting forms were neither men nor selkies.

They were Pili.

The chill that enveloped Kleg had nothing whatever to do with the night winds blowing through the window.

Pili! How could they be here? Surely the

guard would not have admitted an armed band of them! Had they scaled the wall surrounding the village? Broken through the gate?

Never mind that, Kleg. How they got inside is not nearly so important as why they are here: they are after you and not the least doubt of that.

For a moment, Kleg yielded to panic. A score of Pili would move through the village like dung through a worm; it would only take moments for them to find him!

Unbidden, his hand found the pouch of his belt containing the magical talisman. Should they manage to obtain the Seed and somehow spare him, his fate would make a quick death by spear pleasant compared to what He Who Creates would do to him. He had to escape!

Yea, even though it was dark and the weed paths under the water would be most dangerous, he had to get to the lake. In his Changed form, his chances were much better there than in his upright from here. And while the Pili might have managed to breach the village's wall, it would be a cold sun in the desert before they learned how to swim well enough to catch a selkie!

Carefully, Kleg started down the steps.

From below, a voice called out loudly, "We seek a fishman! Is there one here? Speak, or taste my spear!"

"U-u-up-s-stairs," came a quavering response.

Kleg stopped cold. By the Black Depths! He was trapped!

*   *   *

A tall Pili with whom Thayla considered trysting once he got a little older slid down the side of the sand dune from the top and came to rest next to the queen.

"They are coming!" he said.

Thayla nodded. "Exactly as I planned. You know what you are to do."

"Aye, my queen."

"Prepare, then."

The young male nodded and climbed upward, where he rejoined the other two males Thayla had kept with her. The queen herself followed, moving more slowly. She planned to watch from the peak of the hillock as her troops attacked. The numbers on both sides were about equal, but she had the advantage of surprise. Night would help, insofar as confusion went in the dark, but the Pili saw no better than did men, nor was their hearing an improvement.

Well, it did not matter if many or all of her troops died, as long as she got what she wanted.

Now, there was carnage to observe. Doubtless her reptilian ancestors would have been pleased with the smile that thought brought to her lips.

The Queen of the Pili continued to grin as she climbed to a position from which she could watch the slaughter.

*   *   *

Conan slipped away from the others and circled to his right. Perhaps Cheen was right. Perhaps he worried needlessly, like some child afraid of ghosts in the dark. He had seen once again, however, from his confrontation with Crom—if that had been other than a potion-inspired dream—that leaping without looking was fraught with danger. Were it not for that rope about his ankle during the ceremony in the trees, likely his brains would have been dashed all over the roots below. Conan of Cimmeria was not a man to repeat the same mistake once he had grasped the idea of it. One who always used his might and never his wits would likely lead a short life, and he had no intention of so doing.

The sand of the slope was finer than that upon which they had been walking, and Conan stepped upon it carefully to avoid having it cheep birdlike under his sandals. The wind was at his back, and it carried tiny sharp teeth of sand that bit at his exposed flesh and sought to burrow beneath his clothing. The odor of the desert was dry and lifeless, and his nostrils detected no sign of the lizard musk he recalled from the cage and caves.

Halfway up the slope, Conan's sharp blue eyes caught sight of three dark splotches above him, at the peak of the dune. At first he thought the shapes some type of plant, but as he cautiously climbed upward, he realized that he was mistaken.

The three forms were Pili warriors, and they

were intent on something on the other side of
the dune.

Conan could easily guess what that something was: the Tree Folk, walking into a trap.

Taking care to avoid scraping the blade on
the scabbard, the Cimmerian drew his sword.
He was nearly upon the three, who had risen
from prone to half crouches, when the night
wind at his back gave him away.

"Gah, what is that stink?" one of the Pili
answered.

"Not I," a second said.

"It smells familiar," the third said. "Like . . .
it is a man!"

The three started to turn.

No more need for stealth. Conan churned up
the slope, the sand *chee-cheeing* under his
sandals.

He bellowed a warning: "Pili! On the dune
tops! Pili! Beware!"

The yell was replaced by the exclamations of
the startled Pili.

The nearest of the three lunged up, and the
angle of the dune gave him momentum as he
stabbed at Conan with his spear. The Cimmerian
dodged, slow in the dry mire, but quick enough
to avoid the thrust. The Pili's lunge turned into
a fall, then a helpless, uncontrolled tumble as
he flew down the side of the dune, screaming
as he went.

The second Pili managed only to lift his
weapon before Conan's blued-iron blade whistled in the night air and cleaved the lizard man

open from one side of his neck to the opposite shoulder. He sprouted his life's blood into the dry sand, which drank it eagerly.

The third Pili stood to flee, but not fast enough. The point of Conan's sword found and entered the Pili's back and exited through the lizard man's heart and sternum. Conan lifted his right foot and used it to shove the dying Pili from his blade, and this one tumbled down the opposite side of the dune toward the startled Tree Folk below.

Conan took in the scene: the Tree folk, warned by his yell, were already climbing the hill toward him, to take the high ground. Several Pili charged down other dunes, waving spears and yelling. As Conan watched, one of the Tree Folk took a thrown spear in the leg. Little Hok was halfway up the dune by now, with Cheen right behind him. One of the Tree Folk spun and hurled a spear, and was rewarded by a scream from the Pili who caught the point in the belly.

Conan grinned. A simple battle, odds nearly even, now this was something he understood! He yelled wordlessly and charged down the dune, sword raised to smite the enemies below.

THIRTEEN

Kleg searched for options and found them few. Below in the main room of the ramshackle inn, an unknown number of Pili had just discovered his whereabouts. He was on the third floor with only one stairway leading down. He could go down the stairs to a likely death. He could hide and hope to avoid being discovered, or he could develop wings and escape; otherwise he would have to leap to the cobblestones below and that would cost him broken legs at the least and probably worse.

Things did not look promising.

From his belt, Kleg drew the long dagger he habitually carried and resolved to sell his life for as much Pili blood as he could. He did not know if He Who Creates could reach across the death barrier to the Gray Lands, but were such a thing possible, certainly it would happen; did

Kleg die here this night, he meant to show he had struggled valiantly in his master's service before falling.

Suddenly there came a loud crash. The inn shook, as though rattled by an earth tremor, and the voices of those below raised into a frantic, panicked babble. Came up the stairs screams and the sounds of breaking furniture and general chaos.

What in the world . . . ?

Cautiously, Kleg stole down the stairs, dagger in hand.

When he rounded the final turning on the second-story landing, he saw a chair fly past the base of the stairwell, followed by a Pili—sans head.

Something was definitely amiss here.

Kleg descended further, and what he beheld was indeed a frightening sight.

The east wall of the inn was more or less collapsed, the ceiling above canting down over a massive hole to the outside; half a dozen Pili scrabbled around the wrecked room, jabbing their spears at a nightmare.

The monster they fought looked to be part toad, part bear, and perhaps leavened with dog or wolf, but it was huge! Its gaping maw was lined in the front with needlelike teeth that tapered to solid plates of flat molars in the back. The beast chewed something, and Kleg's stomach roiled as he realized that what it chewed was the remains of a Pili's head. The morsel crunched wetly in the monster's jaws.

The jabs of the Pili's spears did not seem to affect it much, if at all, and as Kleg watched, the thing lunged forward, very quickly for such a large creature, and bit the leg from another Pili.

The lizard man screamed, but the beast was apparently as unaffected by this as it was by the spears, which sank into its flesh but drew no blood. The mottled gray-green monster chewed on the leg as a cow chews on her cud, oblivious to all else.

There was a mostly clear pathway to the inn's door, and Kleg decided that there would never be a better time for him to depart. He sprinted toward the exit.

The Pili were too busy to notice him, but Kleg's run did draw the attention of the monster, whose red eyes turned to follow the selkie's dash for freedom.

The knowledge came suddenly to Kleg; the thing was here for *him*!

Certainly the beast was no friend to the Pili. Could it have been sent by the Tree Folk?

Kleg reached the door and ran through it into the street. A small crowd had gathered and was moving toward the inn.

"Hey, whut's alla noise about . . . ?"

". . . god's cursed racket in there . . . ?"

". . . watch it, fool!"

Kleg ignored the people, save for the one he banged into during his flight, and he only paid enough attention to that one to shove him roughly aside. If these idiots wished to enter the inn, so much the better. They would make fodder for the thing therein, and perhaps keep it from following him.

It did not seem likely that the Tree Folk had fielded such a monster, and since it was not one of the Pili's pets, then the logical conclusion was that He Who Creates had sent it. But why? To help Kleg? Or to devour him? Mayhaps the magical talisman that bumped at his waist could survive a trip in the belly of the beast quite easily and that was He Who Creates' intent in sending it.

Kleg did not know the answers to his questions, nor was he interested in waiting here to find out. That hideous monster gobbling up Pili as if they were sweetmeats did not look to be something with which you could reason.

Kleg ran toward the docks, trusting to speed instead of stealth now. If he could but reach the water, he would be safe!

Another thought thrust itself into his consciousness all of a moment. If He Who Creates had sent the beast after him, could not He have also sent others? Things that could even now be waiting in the Sargasso for Kleg?

The running selkie slowed, coming to a stop.

Uh-oh. He could have gone forever without that thought.

Or perhaps not. Perhaps in this case what he did not know *would* hurt him. Perhaps it would *eat* him.

Kleg turned and walked into an alleyway

between a smith's shop and a half-fallen temple. Before he ran pell-mell to the water and threw himself into a set of jaws like those destroying the inn, perhaps he had better think on this for a while.

Rage enveloped Thayla. Her trap was falling apart before her eyes! Someone had given the alarm! The essence of her attack was off, the surprise gone, and even now, the Tree Folk scooted up a dune ahead of her soldiers, largely untouched. Where were the three who were supposed to be at the summit of that hill?

There one of them was—Gods, he was flying down the hill, falling, rolling, and what was—oh, no, it was that barbarian human! He stood there at the crest, waving his sword and yelling. Now he was charging downward, and the Tree Folk were turning to join him.

In the dark, bodies fell, Pili and human; there came the hard clatter of spears, the screams of wounded. And Conan laid about with that sword, chopping her troops down as a Pili clears brush, back and forth, back and forth, by the great Green Dragon.

It was a rout. More Pili were down than men, and whatever advantage the Pili might have had fled like the sand before a windstorm. Another of her troops dropped, cut nearly in half by that berserk man she had taken to her bed. Yet another ate a spear thrown by one of the tree dwellers. Her warriors were the ones being slaughtered, not the men, and Thayla watched in horror as it happened.

It came to her as Conan chased the last of her troops that she herself was in danger. Might not they look for other Pili?

Thayla slid down from her perch on the dune. Best not to be found if they looked.

As she hurried to find a place to hide, the Queen of the Pili was filled with a bitter blend of fear and loathing and anger.

Now what was she going to do?

Conan chased the fleeing Pili and caught him after a short sprint. The heavy iron sword sang a song of death in the night as it chopped the Pili's head from his shoulders. The lizard man collapsed, spouting crimson into the thirsty sands.

The Cimmerian turned, his own blood coursing rapidly within him, searching for more opponents.

Alas, there were no more Pili to be slain.

"Conan, are you unharmed?"

He looked up to see Cheen scurrying toward him.

"Aye. What of the others?"

The two of them began a check of the Tree Folk. They had lost five of their party to Pili spears. A quick count showed nearly a dozen of the lizard men were now corpses.

"Should we search for others?" Hok said to his sister.

"I think not," Cheen said. "Our goal is ahead

and I would not delay here. What say you Conan?"

The Cimmerian was busy with his honing stone, touching up the blade of his sword. As he polished out a nick on the edge with the stone, he nodded at Cheen. "Aye, let us continue onward. It is unlikely that we will be troubled by such as these again." He waved the sharpened sword at the bodies on the sand. "Before the queen realizes we have slain her troops, we will be well out of their territory."

After a quick burial of their dead and attention to the wounds of the living, the group departed the scene of the battle.

Swirling through the quiet halls, Dimma felt within him a sense of frustration. He had done all he could do, he reasoned. His Prime selkie would die before failing, he had sent as much help as was like to be useful, and all he could do now was wait. After five hundred years, a few days was nothing, and yet Dimma could feel the end of his torture almost as if he had flesh and was feeling the touch of a woman. Were he solid, he could venture forth himself, could brave any winds, could go and see for himself what was transpiring. Alas, in his current form, even a stray breeze would drive him before it as a shepherd does lambs, and there was nothing he could do about it, despite his most powerful magicks.

It enraged him, his helplessness, and he

intended to revenge himself upon the world when he again wore the flesh. That he should suffer so for hundreds of years needed payment, and the payment would be in rivers of blood and mountains of bone. Those who had taken their bodies for granted would suffer because he, Dimma, had not been able to enjoy that simple pleasure. Not until his rage was spent would he be content to rest and think about what he would do next.

Now, how would he begin? Well, a plague to kill all the inhabitants of Koth, where a dying wizard's curse had infected Dimma, that would be a good start.

The Mist Mage felt better, thinking about an orgy of destruction. Soon, it would be.

Soon.

Kleg found himself on the horns of a dilemma. On the one side, the village contained Pili who wanted to drink his life and steal the talisman he had stolen, so he had to get to the waters of the lake and the safety of the Sargasso. On the other side of the problem, there was at least one monster after him, and perhaps others, and he was uncertain as to their intent. He Who Creates had motives beyond understanding by a selkie, and the waters might well prove more dangerous than the village.

Kleg leaned against the rough wooden wall of the smith's shop and pondered the problem.

Which was it to be? The demons he knew? Or the demons he did not? One thing for certain, he needed to choose soon. That *thing* might find him again, or the Pili might. Or both unhappy events might come to pass. His chances of surviving such an encounter were slim at best.

Come on, Kleg. Which is it to be?

FOURTEEN

The Queen of the Pili was not one to be discouraged easily. Even though all but one of her troops had been slain—that one spared only because he had been knocked unconscious and was therefore thought dead—Thayla had no intention of giving up the chase. The party of Tree Folk had also lost nearly half its strength, had been reduced to five, not counting Conan and the boy. Seven against two was a situation that precluded direct attack by the smaller number, but despite that, Thayla intended somehow to prevail.

How she was going to see Conan dead was unknown, but some opportunity would arise, of that she was certain.

She and her single trooper, an unseasoned youth called Blad, stayed well back of the Tree Folk as they neared the edge of the desert.

Once they were in the greener land that lay ahead, they could move closer to the others. Perhaps they could pick them off one by one, lowering the odds slowly. Something would occur to her, sooner or later.

Kleg decided. Whatever the possible danger in the lake of his birth, he would be much better equipped to deal with them in his Changed form. That thing back in the inn was larger and more fearsome than a selkie in the water, but given its shape, it could not possibly be as fast. And while there were smaller denizens who could give a swimming selkie pause, there were not many. Better he should be twice his present size and armed with a mouthful of teeth and muscular speed than to be caught here on the shore with nothing but a dagger and these puny land legs. He did not have to take the most direct route to the castle, after all. There were a thousand pathways through the weed.

So be it.

The decision made, Kleg immediately felt better. He worked his way toward the docks, moving in the shadows, taking great care not to be seen. Once he reached the water, it would be but a short swim to the edge of the Sargasso. Yes, this was the wiser decision, to be sure.

As he drew nearer to his goal, Kleg slipped the belt and pouch from his waist, rebuckled the belt, and put it over his head and around his neck. The material of the belt was of some special elastic substance that would easily stretch to accommodate the much-thicker body he wore as a Changed selkie. He Who Creates was nothing if not thorough.

Only a few feet from the water, Kleg patted the pouch around his neck. How light the talisman was; he could hardly tell anything was within the thick leather container. He shook the pouch and listened for the rattle he had grown used to the last few days.

The talisman did not rattle.

Kleg's action only served to cause the flap of the case to gape open. How could that be? He had tied it most securely!

With a sensation of sinking panic, Kleg reached into the leather pouch and groped for the talisman.

And found that it was gone.

The crowd standing on the narrow street in front of the Wooden Fish received a great surprise when, all of a moment, a monster burst through the front door, destroying the portal and bringing half the wall down in the process.

Standing to one side of the gathering was a gnarled man, of boylike stature, named Seihman. He had been strong and adventurous once, but now he was known as Seihman of the swine, for that was his work these days, to care for the boars and sows owned by one of the village's richer men. Hardly a glorious function, but it kept him in food and wine—mostly wine—and was certainly better than starving—or worse, dying of thirst.

When the hideous beast broke through the wall of the inn, Seihman's reaction matched that of the rest of the curious: he turned to flee. Around him, the crowd broke like a fat raindrop striking a smooth stone. Seihman, whose best years were long past, ran for all he was worth, trying to watch the demon or whatever at the same time. His initial burst of speed was quite remarkable in that it was unmatched by any younger man on the street; alas, Seihman managed only three such quick bounds before he stepped upon something hard and roundish, tripped, and fell flat on his back.

The crowd vanished like smoke in a high wind, and Seihman found himself sprawled alone on the street altogether too close to a creature large enough to swallow him in one gulp, had it a mind to do so.

"Mitra, spare me!"

Seihman had not spent a copper or a moment in one of Mitra's temples in twenty winters, but he inwardly swore to make amends for this lack if only the Divine One would see fit to allow him this one small favor.

The beast, as ugly a thing as Seihman had ever beheld, glanced without apparent interest at the fallen man, then turned and trotted off down the street toward the lake.

Seihman managed to sit up. "Oh, blessings on you, Divine Mitra! I am in your debt!"

As the monster ambled away from him, Seihman chanced to look down to see what had tripped him.

What was this here odd-looking eye-shaped thing? Some kind of pit, much larger than any he had ever seen, though. A seed?

Seihman gingerly picked up the Seed and hefted it in one hand. Maybe it had some value? Standing, he put the Seed inside his ragged tunic, where it rested warmly against the skin of his aged belly. He would take it by Old Talow, the vegetable merchant. Maybe Talow might recognize it, and who knowed? Maybe he would even buy it. Could be it might be worth a mug of cheap wine, maybe.

Before the curious could return, Seihman shuffled off toward his lodging behind the swine pens. He began to spin a story in his mind to tell his friend the goatherd over a mug of wine when next they met: Aye, I did see the thing what wrecked the Wooden Fish. Come right at me, it did, but I stood my ground all alone and stared it down, and it turned tail and runned off.

Well. It was almost true.

Dawn broke cloudless, splashing the land next to the river with pale and cool sunshine.

The recent rains had washed out most of the tracks of the fleeing selkies, but when Conan and the Tree Folk reached the bank of a rushing river, they found ample evidence of the fishmen.

Lying on the shore were five or six dead selkies, of two versions: one like those Conan had seen at the trees, only these were bloated and purple and covered with buzzing flies. The other version of selkie was a great fish twice the size of a man, with an underslung jaw full of teeth and a smooth, tapering body with long fins and tail. These also were swollen in death, fly-blown, and two of the corpses had small spears lodged in them. The air stank of poison, and this was confirmed by the fact that no scavengers had been at the meat and fish. The flies, too stupid to know better, ate and died by the hundreds.

"Hie, look here!" Hok called.

Conan moved to where the boy stood. Hok pointed down at tracks in the drying mud. Conan recognized them from his time in the desert. Pili.

Well. It took no genius to understand what had happened here. The Pili and the selkies had fought, and it seemed that the Pili had gotten at least a few of the fishmen.

Cheen came to stand next to Conan. "There are some dead Pili farther downstream," she said.

"And it looks as if there are more Pili tracks on the other side of the river, though it's hard to say from here," the Cimmerian said.

"You have good eyes," Cheen said.

"We should make a raft and cross. There, on the opposite side, someone else has already done so." He pointed at a wooden platform beached slightly downstream.

Cheen said, "Aye, that has the look of our construction. Tair is still ahead of us."

"Best we move to catch him."

"You do not think there are any more like these in the water, do you?" She pointed at one of the great fish, then shuddered.

"Likely not. No reason for them to stay, if any survived."

They set about building a raft, a chore that took not as long as Conan would have supposed. The Tree Folk were very good with wood and vine, and in a matter of hours, they were done.

The crossing was uneventful.

"Another day's travel and we should arrive at a village on the shore of the Sargasso lake," Cheen said as they disembarked from the raft.

"So I have been told. I have never been there myself."

"And past that?"

"The Mist Mage lives in the weed. He has a floating castle in the middle. No one has ever gone there and returned, save his creatures."

"Best hope we catch the selkies before then," Conan said.

"Aye."

Thayla and Blad counted the dead Pili they found along the riverbank. There were at least a dozen, and the Dragon knew how many more might have been washed downstream out of sight. That fool, her husband, did not seem to be among the corpses. Thayla was unsure of how to react to this. While Blad moaned over dead comrades, Thayla felt that the discovery was somewhat a mixed blessing. Had the king been among the fallen, her chase would have been over. She would be queen, could choose some pliant male as consort—maybe even Blad here—and live out her days in what luxury she could force from the Pili.

But as long as Rayk lived, there existed the chance that he would find out about Conan. Of course, she had survived such rumors before, because the transgressor in question had always been devoured and therefore had been unable to answer any questions about the matter. Even a fool expected no reply from a boiling pot of soup. But Conan lived, and as long as he and her husband both continued to do so, she was in peril.

"We need a raft," Thayla told Blad. "Construct one so that we may cross."

"At once, my queen."

"You need your strength now," she said, smiling at the young male, "but after we cross the river, perhaps I can find a way to suitably reward you for your steadfast service, Blad my worthy." Might as well bind him to her personally, she decided.

The young male stared at her. "I need no reward, milady."

Thayla shrugged out of her heavy travel robe, then quickly removed her undergarments. After a moment, she stood naked before him. "But you shall have one anyway. If you hurry."

As she redressed, Thayla smiled and thought to herself that never had she seen a Pili move with such alacrity.

Where was the talisman?

That was the question that filled Kleg's mind to bursting. How could it have been lost? When? Where?

As he made his way back toward the inn, he went over in his mind for the hundredth time all the events and places of the last day. He had still had the talisman in the room he had taken for sleeping. He had opened the pouch to check. Somehow, he had failed to secure the leather strings properly, and somehow, the magic Seed had fallen from its container.

Had it been during the run downstairs? Or when he had seen that beast? Or when ... ?

Wait. He had bumped into somebody on the street, some fool gawking at the inn, he had shoved the man aside—

Yes! That was it! He must have flung the talisman loose during that encounter.

In the dark, perhaps no one had noticed it. It was not remarkable to look upon, a brownish gray, mostly round, and pointed-on-both-ends seed, looking like nothing so much as a giant fruit pit.

With the coming of daylight, however, someone might notice the Seed.

Kleg moved quickly, but he kept to alleyways

and next to buildings as much as possible. Dawn brought an end to the shadows in which he had hidden from the Pili, and there were at least a few who had not met their end at the jaws of the beast. Of course, they should not be inside the village, so they would also have to be less than obvious in their movements. A single Pili here and there would likely raise a few eyebrows but no real alarm. Half a dozen spear-bearing lizard men marching abreast would have the local guard out in a hurry, and they had to know that.

The Prime selkie crossed a narrow side road, moving quickly past an old man throwing grain into a penful of swine. The old man stared, but Kleg did not speak or slow his pace.

And what of that monster? What had happened to it? He had not seen it again during his dodgings, but he doubted that the creature had been slain by the Pili, or by anybody else.

Ah, this was all becoming too complicated. He had to find that talisman, and he had to find it quickly!

Seihman looked up from his strewing of near-fermented grain to the pigs to see the selkie march past. The old man shook his head. Strange goings-on about here of late. There was that demon thing in the street, this selkie, and early this morning, when the cock still crowed, he had seen one of them lizard men skulking about, too. It added up to a bad omen, he reckoned, and best he step lightly so as not to get stuck in the middle of whatever was going on.

He tossed the final bucket of slops to the pigs, dropped the wooden container next to the rail fence, and figured it was time to go and get something to drink for breakfast. The goatherder ought to be coming round about now, and maybe he could get a bit of free wine out of him with the story about the monster.

Oh, and that pit he had found, maybe he could take that by Old Talow's and get a copper or two for it.

Seihman reached inside his shirt for the seed.

Whups. Not there. Hmm. Musta dropped it somewheres. Ah, well, no help for it. Probably not worth anything, anyways.

FIFTEEN

Kleg could not recall a worse day in his life. The time He Who Creates caught him with the kitchen maid had been bad, as had the occasion when he accidentally ripped a thousand-year-old tapestry down from one of the castle walls. This, however, made those as nothing.

He had returned to the street outside the destroyed tavern. The monster was gone, fortunately. Unfortunately, the magic talisman was also absent. If he had in fact dropped the item in the street—and he could not think otherwise—then somebody or some*thing* had picked it up.

The sun's light slanted down from on high, and Kleg could not tarry for fear of being spotted by the Pili. He had seen a pair of them lurking behind a shed earlier, but luckily they had not been aware of him.

The selkie leaned against the back wall of the

Wooden Fish, hidden in a patch of thick shade. What was he going to do? To return to face He Who Creates without the talisman meant a painful, messy death, and no doubt of that. To *fail* to return would hardly be better. Kleg knew that no matter how fast or how far he ran, he could not escape the vengeance of his master. He could put off the inevitable for a time, but as sure as the sun went down each night so would Kleg go down, and if his death for failure would be bad, his end for trying to get away would be thrice as horrible, were such a thing possible. He Who Creates had raised the selkies from the slime of the lake bottom and made them stronger and faster than the men who ruled most of the earth. One who could turn bottom fish into selkies with a wave of His hand could certainly find one of His creations and squash him as easily as a child could squash a bothersome gnat.

No, neither of those options offered the Prime selkie the slightest joy.

The only road to redemption was the road that led to the talisman. But how? He could hardly walk around asking every passerby if he had happened to find a magic Seed stolen from the Tree Folk, now, could he? And mayhaps the Pili had already found it.

Kleg shook his head. Why had he been put in this position? All he asked from life was to be allowed access to females and game fish! It was hardly fair. He had done what he was supposed to do. Surely He Who Creates, Who Knew All, could see that?

Aye. And perhaps this was part of the test. To see how hard His servant would strive to accomplish his given task.

Kleg shook his head again. Why me?

Evening began drawing her black cloak about the land when Conan and his party finally caught up with Tair and the second group of Tree Folk. There was some rejoicing to see those still living, and also sorrow for those who had perished along the way.

As the two small units of Tree Folk mingled, Conan stood apart. Not far from them, a huge black rock lay embedded in the earth, as if dropped by the hand of a careless god.

The greetings and commiserations done, Tair and Cheen came to stand next to Conan.

"The village of Karatas lies just beyond the black rock," Tair said. "The last of the selkies have attained sanctuary there. There was a battle at a river a ways back, between the selkies and a large group of Pili."

"Aye," Conan said, "we saw signs of it."

"Apparently the Pili also chased the selkies. Somehow, they, too, have managed to get inside the walls surrounding the village."

"Then that is where we must go."

Tair nodded. "Aye, but there is a problem. Due to some trouble, the normal gate guard has been trebled, and they are allowing no strangers to enter. Even one who is as brave and strong as I cannot hope to break through the entrance."

Conan shrugged. "So we find another way to get inside."

"I am given to understand that the walls of Karatas have not been breached since they were built," Cheen said. "Some have tried."

"I did not offer to breach them," Conan said. "Do you not think that you can climb them?"

Tair grinned widely and slapped Conan on one hard shoulder. "By the Green Goddess, surely you jest? There is nothing I cannot climb!"

"And the others?"

"Well, they are not so adept as I, certainly, but a wall of wood can hardly offer much challenge. The palisade is, after all, nothing more than a bunch of trees without limbs."

"Then we should find an unwatched spot and climb," Conan said. "When darkness is the deepest."

"Aye, a clever idea. We can drop a line for you once we are atop the wall."

"I think I can manage the climb on my own."

Aye, he thought, or die trying before allowing himself to be pulled up on a rope. The Tree Folk had no more fingers or toes than did Cimmerians, and if they could scale that wall, he would be cursed forever if he could not do the same.

"I shall send a scout to find a good place,"

Tair said. "Meanwhile, let us eat and speak of our adventures. I have much to say."

Conan grinned. Aye, he was certain of that fact. Never had he met a people so full of themselves. They had raised the standards of bragging, to be sure.

Thayla chewed on a hard root and grimaced at the taste and texture. There was some milky fluid in the thing that spurted into her mouth, producing a salty and slightly bitter tang. While sustaining, it was hardly part of a diet she would desire given choice. Still, one had to make do. There was no time to hunt meat and still maintain their watch on the Tree Folk and that accursed Conan.

Next to her under the cover of thick shrubbery, Blad smiled at her. Simpleton that he was, he required very little to make him happy. After crossing the river where so many of their kind had died, Thayla had gifted the young Pili with a treasure he had never thought to attain, and now he belonged to her, body and spirit. Males were so predictable it was laughable.

"They are settled, you say?"

"Aye, milady. They eat and talk among themselves."

Thayla digested this bit of information along with another bit of root. Whatever idea she had had about slaying the Tree Folk one at a time vanished when Conan and his group joined another, larger band of the accursed humans. There were nearly a score of them gathered together now, and a misstep on Blad's part would likely see him skewered. Not that such an idea greatly distressed her, since she thought of males as disposable—one Pili was as good as another; they all looked alike under the moon— but since Blad here was the only one she had, Thayla was loath to give him up—at least until she had a suitable replacement.

"We are near the village?" she said.

"Aye, my queen. A few minutes' walk."

What, she wondered, were the Tree Folk up to now? And where was that fool husband of hers? The village squatted on the edge of a vast lake, and he had to be inside the walls—unless he was in the water or somehow on the weed therein, neither of which she thought likely. So what was he doing in there?

"Go and watch the men," Thayla ordered. "Report back immediately if anything happens."

The smile vanished from Blad's face. Doubtless he had something other in mind than lying alone in the brush spying on their quarry. Thayla reached out and stroked his arm. She gave him a half-lidded look and a sultry smile. "I shall wait here for your return."

The grin blossomed again on Blad's face and he jumped up almost eagerly. "At once, my queen!"

After he was gone, Thayla shook her head. Truly males were driven by something other than their brains.

*   *   *

The thick of night found Kleg sitting unhappily in a rat-infested tavern near the docks. A sign outside proclaimed the tavern to be the Bright Hope. The name was a huge joke, for there was neither brightness nor hope within.

Kleg brooded over a wooden cup of kral under the flickering light of sputtering fat lamps. The rough, filthy room was filled with smoke and perhaps a score of low-caste men and half as many bottom-of-the-barrel trulls seeking to service them. The planks of the walls were warped and colored a dead gray, with torn fishnets draped here and there as an attempt at decorations. A vile place. Kleg was only in it because he thought it unlikely anyone would think to look for him here.

Kleg sipped at his drink. The crowd of men was a rough one, cutpurses, dock thugs, and the like, with a thin leavening of more upright citizens: at a table near the selkie, a goatherder and a swinekeeper drunkenly told each other tales in loud voices.

None of the riffraff bothered Kleg. It was well known that a selkie was no easy mark, being stronger than a man even on land and quick to anger if irritated. Small consolation.

". . . No, wait, let me tell ye about the time I slew a direwolf with naught else but my sling—"

"No, no, no, I heared that story a hundred times! Let me tell you o' the monster at the inn!"

The goatherder splashed wine down the front of his already-stained and stinking sheepskin jerkin. "Ah, go on with ye, it's lies ye be tellin'!"

"No, no, no! I was there, I tell you! It come right through the wall o' the Fish, tore the wood like it was a spider's web and come right at me! Big as a house"—Here the swinekeeper waved his mug of wine to emphasize the size of the thing about which he spoke, and sloshed a goodly portion of the wine into a high arc that ended on the dirt floor—"it were, and me standin' there in the street all alone, nothin' between it 'n' me, and I says to myself, by Mitra, my time is come, so's I might as well go out like a man. I stared it in the eye, I did, I dared it to come for me, and it see'd my face and turned away!"

"Aye, I'ud run were I sober and seeing you for the first time meself," the goatherder said. Amused at his own joke, the man laughed loudly, trailing off into a hoarse cackle.

"No! I faced 'im down, I did! The street were thick with folk and they every one of 'em ran like water bugs from a carp! But I stood my ground! I'ud show you, it ever comes back, the demon!"

This brought another round of raspy cackles.

Kleg was distracted by his plight, else he would have picked up on the substance of the conversation sooner. As it was, he realized the implications as the goatherder stood and made some comment about emptying his bladder, then stumbled off, weaving awkwardly through the clutter of the room.

If any of this were true, if this old man had been on the street when the monster broke out of the inn last eve, then maybe he had seen the talisman!

Kleg shook his head. It was a faint hope. Still, a faint hope was better than no hope at all.

The selkie stood and moved toward the old swinekeeper.

Even through his drunken haze, the man's face registered his fear as Kleg loomed over him.

"Eh?"

"I heard part of your story," Kleg said. "A man as brave as you deserves more than scorn. What are you drinking?"

"Why, dregwine, what else?"

Kleg waved at the serving woman, a white-haired slattern dressed in a shapeless rag whose original color had become hidden under layers of filth. "Ho, a bottle of your best for my brave friend here."

The swinekeeper's face lit up with besotted joy. "Why, that's kind o' you, milord! You bein' a selkie and all, not that I ever had any disrespect for your kind, you unnerstand."

Kleg nodded. "Tell of this adventure of yours of which I have heard so much talk."

"Much talk, eh? Ha, shows what that fool goatherd knows! Aye, milord, it were a terrible sight! Only last night it happened."

The wizened little man launched into a re-telling of the story Kleg had overheard. He paused when the serving woman returned with the wine, poured until his cup overflowed, and drank half the new portion. "Aye, so there I were, all alone, facing the demon with naught but my courage. . . ."

A hush fell over the room, the conversations around stopping as if by a signal. Kleg glanced up from the old man's rambling, to see what had caused the sudden quiet.

Standing in the doorway, outlined by the fat lamps to either side of the entrance, was a Pili.

The swinekeeper was oblivious and had grown more heroic in his retelling his tale.

". . . so I moved toward it, figurin' to poke its eye out, maybe . . ."

The Pili could hardly see much in the smoky room, Kleg felt, but if he came in and allowed his eyes to adjust to the gloom, it would not be long before he would be able to pick out the only selkie therein.

Kleg surreptitiously fingered his knife. One-on-one, he felt that he could hold his own, especially with surprise on his side.

The Pili strode into the room. No one spoke, save the drunken swinekeeper, who was lost in his own glory. Then a second Pili entered, followed by a third.

Uh-oh. This altered things.

"We are searching for one of the fishmen," the lead Pili said.

Fully half of the room's patrons turned to look at Kleg.

The Pili took note of the action, and his gaze followed the others to where Kleg sat.

"Ah! At last!"

But whatever else the Pili would have said or done to Kleg at that moment was lost in the sound of the east wall being rent. A fat lamp flew and splashed burning fuel over men and rude furniture as the wall splintered inward. Men screamed and scrambled to run. The building shook as if swatted by a giant's hand, and the froglike monster of which the drunk next to Kleg spoke burst through the wood as if indeed the wall were no stronger than the web of a garden spider.

The swinekeeper, who, in his tale, was now *chasing* this same creature through the streets of the village, took one look at the snorting apparition that had just chewed through the wall and fainted dead away.

The three Pili could not stand against the panic of thirty men. The lizards were swept through the doorway by the stampede. The dry wood began to burn where the fat lay upon it.

Kleg grabbed up the unconscious swinekeeper and carried the man after the others. He spared a glance backward ... to see that the monster was right behind him. He ran harder, dodging and twisting through the dingy alleys of the village.

SIXTEEN

Time and weather had not treated the palisade surrounding the village particularly well. Perhaps climbing the wall would have seemed difficult to an ordinary man, but Conan found the task relatively simple. Rot had invaded many spots, and digging the punk from the decayed areas produced more than adequate hand and footholds. Where the wood had resisted one enemy, others could be found: wormholes, bird attacks, termites, all contributed to Conan's ease of ascent. They might as well have hung a ladder over the parapet. If these people depended upon their wall as the major deterrent against outsiders, then they were living in a fool's realm.

For all his skill as a Cimmerian, Conan moved slowly compared to the Tree Folk. They swarmed up the wall as might ants, moving as quickly and certainly as a man hurrying down a wide garden path.

Once over the wall, Conan rejoined the others.

"Now what?" Cheen asked.

"Now we go hunting for selkies," Conan said. "Small groups, no more than two or three, so as not to attract attention."

"I shall go with you," Cheen said.

"Very well. Should any of the couples discover our quarry, best they send for help."

After the remainder of the Tree Folk divided up, they started into the strangely quiet village.

Conan led Cheen down an alley, moving toward what he thought the center of the small town. Now, were he a selkie, where would he be?

The answer to that was plain: in the water and on my way back to the magician who had sent me. Still, the obvious was not always the answer. Had the selkies attained the water and the mat of weed, then pursuit was likely ended, according to what Cheen said. Conan did not wish to be another of the men who ventured to the wizard's castle and failed to return. The life of the trees hung in the balance, but when he compared it to his own life, the Cimmerian youth was pragmatic. There were other trees, albeit none so large, that Cheen and her kind could learn to inhabit. As far as he knew, there was only one Conan of Cimmeria, and he meant to keep that one alive.

He stopped and sniffed the air.

"What is it?" Cheen asked.

"Something is burning."

"Aye, probably a hundred fireplaces and five times that many grease lamps and tapers," she said. "The stench is quite obvious."

"No, it is more than that. And listen."

Cheen cocked her head to one side. "I hear only the wind from the lake, and some night bird—wait. Voices."

Conan nodded. Aye, voices, and under that, the crackle of a fire, a fairly big one.

He looked up at the low clouds, casting his gaze back and forth. "There," he said, pointing.

A faint orange flicker danced on the clouds. "What is it?"

"The clouds reflect the fire. Let us go and see what fuels it."

He led Cheen unerringly toward the source of the fire.

When the Cimmerian and the woman from the trees arrived, the conflagration had already drawn a sizable crowd. A hundred or more people stood about, watching the building burn. As Conan drew to a halt, he saw the flames leap to the roof of the structure next to the one already burning. A collective gasp arose from the crowd, followed by a babble of excited voices.

A line of a dozen men bearing sloshing buckets appeared. One by one, the men darted toward the flames and hurled the contents of their containers at the burning buildings. It was to little avail, Conan saw. The heat was too great for the firefighters to approach too closely, and probably half the water splashed short, landing on the street. What fluid reached the flames had little, if any, effect.

The firefighters ran off to fetch more water.

Standing a few feet away, a man dressed in a goatherder's fleece and smelling of his charges talked to no one in particular.

"Mitra strike me down if I lie, but old Seihman 'uz right. Knocked a hole right in the wall, the beast did, an' it be a monster right enough!" The goatherder shook his head. "Ye ne'er see'd nothin' like it! I leaves to visit the night chamber and when I gets back, there be a room full o' lizard men, fishmen, and monsters eatin' right through the stinkin' walls!"

Conan shifted a few steps to face the old man.

"Fishmen, you say?"

"Aye, one o' 'em, anyways. Sittin' right there big as you please next to old Seihman himself and drinkin' wine when the thing come through the wall! Snatched up old Seihman and run off."

"To where?"

The goatherder glanced up from his drunken gaze at Conan's chest. "Mitra, you're a big 'un, ain'tcha?"

"The fishman, where did he go?"

The goatherder shook his head. "Dunno. Like to got trampled, I 'uz too busy to see wheres they got to."

"How long ago?"

"Since the fire. Not long."

Conan turned away from the man and looked at Cheen. "Like as not our quarry," he said.

"What of the beast of which he spoke?" Cheen asked.

Conan shrugged. "What of it? No concern of ours. We should look for the fishmen. There cannot be too many selkies around here carrying old men. He should not be too hard to find. Come."

As the pair turned away, the fire spread to another building. The crowd gasped.

"My queen, the men are leaving!"

Thayla was thus roused from a light sleep. "What?"

"They move toward the village," Blad said.

"But you said the gate was guarded."

"So it is. They are not going toward the gate."

Thayla shook her head, trying to clear the dregs of slumber. "Show me."

She followed the young male toward the village. The trip was a short one, and she arrived in time to see the tree dwellers and Conan scaling the wall.

"They are audacious," she said.

"What are we to do now, milady?"

"Follow them. If they can climb it, so can we."

Indeed, it was so. While it took a considerable effort and no small amount of time, Thayla, aided by Blad, managed to surmount the wall, using finger and toeholds invisible from a distance.

By the time the two Pili had managed the task, the Tree Folk and Conan were not to be seen.

Thayla felt a moment of panic. If her husband still lived, it was very likely that he, too, was in this collection of detritus that passed for a human town, and it was not so large a place that the King of the Pili might never bump into her barbarian lover. She had to find Conan before this happened and see him dispatched to meet with his gods. But where was he?

"Look, milady. Smoke."

Aye, there was a thick curl of dark smoke in the air, and beyond it, a flicker of red orange that could only be flame. Would not a fire draw Conan's attention as well?

"Let us go there," she said.

Kleg was in a panic as he ran, carrying the drunken old man who smelled of swine and had lapsed into unconsciousness. There could be no doubt that the monster that ate its way through the second building in which the selkie had been had come looking for him. How had it found him? Well, were it sent by He Who Creates, such a problem was no more than a trifle. This thought only confirmed Kleg's thoughts as to his master's relative omnipotence.

He had to find the talisman and he had to get back to the castle and he had to do both quickly. One could not dodge such enemies as the Pili and a magical beast forever in a village bounded by walls on three sides and water on the other—

Hsst! What was this?

Kleg slid into a patch of dark shadow next to a bakery and stared at two figures in the narrow street just beyond. There was a man and a small boy, dressed in the style of the Tree Folk, standing under the fitful light of a dying torch. He could not be sure, but the boy looked familiar. Of course, they all looked alike to Kleg, but—could this not be the image of the boy he had traded to the Pili for passage?

No, he decided, it could not be. That particular boy would have been stew long ago, a morsel to be consumed quickly by the rapacious Pili.

No matter. What *did* matter was that the two were most certainly Tree Folk, and—how had they gotten here? Were their others of their kind? Yes, yes, there must be. And that they were after Kleg he doubted not a whit.

By the Black Depths! It was not enough to be chased by two kinds of enemy; now there were three!

Kleg sagged. It was most unfair.

He turned and sprinted into the nearby alleyway to avoid the tree dwellers. He had to get to a place where he could revive this smelly pig man and find out what he knew. If, Kleg worried, the old man knew anything useful at all.

After a series of dodges and twists, the Prime

selkie found a leather stable that, save for two
spavined horses, was empty. The gloom inside
was unbroken, save for a high window that
admitted enough night light so that he could
barely see. Kleg dropped the old man on a
mound of dry hay, inhaled the dusty scent
kicked up by the action, and began searching
for something with which to revive the drunk.

He found a leather bucket used to feed the animals, and scooped it full of scummy water from a
trough. Returning to the old man, the selkie
dribbled some of the warm liquid onto his face.
When this provoked no response, he upended
the bucket and dumped all the contents into
the old man's face. That woke him up.

"Hey! Leave off! Mitra curse you!"

Kleg waited as the old man wiped his face
with his bony hands.

"Who are you?"

"I bought you wine, remember?"

"Oh. In the Bright Hope. The fishman. Why
is it so dark in here, I cannot see."

"That does not matter now. Recall the beast
that attacked you in the street last eve?"

"My head hurts. I need a drink."

"Later. You shall have a barrel of wine, if
you aid me."

"Eh? A barrel o' wine?"

"When you saw the beast last night, did you
happen to notice anything else?"

"Anything else? Such as?"

"A . . . seed. About the size of a man's fist."

"Aye, I did see such a thing. Picked it up,

I did, I meant to sell it to the old Talow, but . . ."

"But what?"

In the semidarkness, Kleg could see the old man's features grow crafty, his bloodshot eyes narrowing, his lips curling into a thin smile.

"Go on, about the Seed."

"Well, maybe it has got some value, eh?"

"I have already said, a barrel of wine if you can produce it."

"Maybe more than a barrel o' wine, eh? Maybe it is worth two barrels?"

"Two, done."

"Ah. Three, maybe?"

The selkie's anger enveloped him like a shroud. Every other soul on the streets wished to drink his blood and this stinking old man wanted to exact a higher price! Kleg grabbed the old man's ragged shirtfront with one hand and lifted him clear off the floor; with his other hand, he drew his knife and laid the point against the man's wrinkled throat. "And maybe I shall cut your head off and spit down the hole! If you have the Seed, produce it!"

"N-n-no, don't cut me! I-I-I d-don't have it—"

Kleg pressed the tip of the knife against the flesh and a bead of blood appeared.

"W-w-wait! I had it! B-b-b-but I lost it!"

"Where did you lose it?"

"I d-d-dunno. I had it wh-when I slopped the pigs this morning! Then I could not find it!"

"Where are the animals penned?"

"B-behind the sl-sl-slaughterhouse! Two st-streets up fr-from the g-g-grain b-b-bin."

Kleg lowered the old man, so that he stood on shaky legs. "Is this true? Could you have dropped it at the pens?"

"Y-yes. I am sure that is wh-where I lost it."

Kleg felt a surge of hope within his breast. Could it be that he might still find the talisman and escape?

"What of my wine?" the old man said. His voice had lost its quaver and greed had replaced the fear.

Kleg looked at the old man. He could not have this drunken lout telling this tale to anyone else.

"The wine. Ah, yes. It is right there, behind you."

When the old man turned around to squint into the darkness, Kleg grabbed his hair with one hand and drew the sharp blade across his throat, hard. The old man gurgled and pitched forward, clutched at his neck, and tried to dam the outward flow of his life. He failed.

Kleg noticed that it was getting lighter inside. He glanced at the window and saw that the sky was a glowing yellow orange. The fire, it must be spreading!

The selkie did not spare the swinekeeper a backward glance as he darted from the stable.

By the Black Depths, half the village was in flames!

He had to get to the swine pens before the whole place went up.

He ran.

Conan realized that they were in danger when he saw a building next to the palisade collapse and fall against the wall. Flames licked at the wooden retainer, and in moments it, too, was being eaten by the raging fire.

Conan grabbed Cheen by one arm. "We must get out of the village!"

"What?"

"The fire is out of control, the whole town is going to burn. We will be cooked in here!"

Around them, people began to realize much the same thing, judging from the excited tones of their voices. Conan watched as a group of four men ran down the main street toward the main gate in the distance. Flaming structures lined both sides of the road, and when the four were only a hundred paces away, the tallest of the buildings lurched forward and fell, covering the men with burning wood and blocking the street with more fire.

The fires reached up toward the night sky as more and more buildings took light. The heat smote Conan on his exposed skin. The very air was hot in his lungs. Buildings exploded into flame now, popping and crackling and swirling like dust devils.

Screams filled the air as the inhabitants realized how bad it really was. A wall of mad, dancing fire sprang up, blocking any exit **toward the village gate, and even the palisade** itself now shot fiery fingers even higher, driving the darkness well back.

"The lake," Conan said. "We must go toward the lake."

"The lake is dangerous!"

"It is certain death any other way! Come!"

The two of them turned and ran in the direction of the only coolness left in the village. And even attaining that was not assured, as the pitch-covered docks sunk in the lake were beginning to smolder in places.

Conan looked up to see a Pili running the same way, and next to the lizard man, he spotted Tair and Hok, also fleeing. Whatever differences any of them had would have to wait, for when fleeing fire, all animals were brothers.

SEVENTEEN

Thayla went from worrying about her husband to worrying about being roasted. Almost everywhere she looked flames filled the night. The whole village was on fire! What was going on here?

"Milady! This way!"

For a moment, Thayla allowed herself to be pulled along by Blad; he seemed to know where he was going. Then she saw an opening in the wall of fire, and she shouted at him. "That way is clear."

"That leads to the lake, milady!"

She took his point. Pili did not swim, there being little opportunity to do so in the desert. Then again, while the desert was hot, it hardly compared to a raging fire.

"There will be water craft of some kind. Hurry!"

They hurried. The crackle of light and heat was joined here and there by the collapse of buildings and the screams of villagers too slow to escape one or the other.

Thayla did not know what had caused the inferno but she suspected that her quarry had been in some way responsible.

The Queen of the Pili dodged a shower of flaming embers falling in her path. Time to worry about cause later, fool. Worry about escape now!

As the Mist Mage floated down one of the many corridors of his enclosed realm, he felt himself grow heavy. Could it be? Could he be about to gain solidity again, so soon?

With that very thought, he coalesced into the substance of a man and dropped to the stone floor.

A miracle! For this to happen again so soon after the last time surely must portend good fortune? His goal must be nearly attained!

None of his servants were near, and he needed to get to food and his mistress while he wore the flesh. So Dimma ran down the hall, glorying in his ability to do so. As he passed a thick sheet of quartz that had been carved into a bat-shaped window and inset into the wall to admit light, he skidded to a stop. He very nearly fell, being unused to walking, much less running, but managed to maintain his footing. He returned to the window and stared through it.

The quartz was of varying thickness, so that anything viewed through it was somewhat distorted to a man's eye, but the mineral was of sufficient quality to allow Dimma to see in the distance, on a clear day, the village of Karatas, on the eastern edge of the lake. Under night's shroud as it now was, the village was usually invisible, the tiny lights being too far away to be viewed. But Dimma could see it now, Karatas. Or what was left of it.

Even from so great a distance, the flames that engulfed the town formed a bright flickering that lit the night.

Dimma stared at the sight. In his five hundred years, he had seen many towns destroyed—by wind, by fire, sometimes by magic. After such a long time, little surprised him. Some fool of a peasant knocks over a lamp and the tinder-dry wood of his hut catches the sizzling oil and ignites, spreading to other hovels quickly. All too common a happening.

Still, as Dimma watched, a grin lit his face. Even though it was a sight he had seen many times, it was not one of which he had ever tired. The villagers' terror would be a delicious morsel, could he but be close enough to hear their frightened yells, could he but see their stricken faces. Ah, yes, some things never lost their appeal.

But as Dimma continued his vigil, he felt a ratlike worry gnawing at his thoughts. His Prime selkie would most likely come through the village on his way back with the final ingredient of Dimma's salvation. Had he already completed his passage, there was no problem. Or, had Kleg yet to reach the town on the shore, he could wait for it to finish burning, also without any danger, a delay Dimma did not like, but could understand. But what if Kleg were *in* the village even as Dimma watched? What if the fool allowed himself to be consumed by the fire, and with him the only remaining piece of the spell Dimma needed to remove his curse?

No, that would not do, not at all!

Dimma turned away from the quartz window and sought to run again. He would send more of his thralls to look for the selkie. Every beast under his command, if need be, for nothing was more important than that this quest be ended successfully, nothing!

Dimma managed five quick steps, but the sixth was denied him. As his foot reached for the floor, the Mist Mage lost himself. As he became brother to smoke once again, Dimma screamed his frustration to the heavens.

Kleg, Prime selkie, highest of those brought up from the fishes by He Who Creates, knelt in mud thick with swine excrement, digging through it with his hands.

The pigs were gone. Kleg had knocked the fence aside, and the squealing animals fled the approaching fire without so much as a backward glance. The selkie himself glanced nervously over his shoulder now and again. That cursed monster could appear again at any moment, but he could not allow himself to dwell on it.

Already, the mud began to dry from the intense heat, making it more difficult to work. The nearest building had not yet taken flame, but it smoked and creaked next to him, and it would only be a matter of moments before it joined the storm of flames that beat at the night.

He had not much time left, Kleg knew. Flames ate the village around him, he was very nearly encircled, and the skin on his arms and face baked under the approaching enemy's hot breath. He dragged his fingers through the mud like small rakes, praying that the old man had spoken the truth. It had to be here. It *had* to be!

A loud *pop!* announced the ignition of the building next to Kleg. The blast of heat smote at the selkie like a hot fist.

Kleg dived away, sprawling facedown in the mud. The muck was cooling to his skin, and he quickly rolled onto his back, coating himself with a thick layer there as well. That helped, but he knew it would only buy him a few seconds. He had to flee now, or die.

There was no help for it, the talisman was lost.

Kleg took two steps through the hardening mire and put his foot down on something hard.

He dropped and dug through the sty. His hand touched a familiar shape. Could it be?

The Seed!

Kleg grinned as he dug the talisman from the mud. He had it!

He stuffed the muddy Seed into his pouch, made certain that the pouch was tied securely shut this time, and ran. The corridor ahead narrowed rapidly, but he was through before the fire claimed it completely.

Ahead, the smell of the lake called. The fire was nearly everywhere, but Kleg was certain he could make it to the water and the weed beyond.

With the mud protecting him against the intense heat, Kleg dodged his way toward safety.

Conan led Cheen, Tair, and Hok to the edge of the lake. Others of the village had much the same idea, and the Cimmerian and his small band arrived at the shore next to a collection of small boats and pulled up on the mud at the same time as a dozen villagers.

Conan moved toward a boat that would hold six people safely.

A large man beat him to it. "This 'un is mine!" the man said. He started to shove the boat into the water.

"There is room for half a dozen. We will share it," Conan said.

"Nay! There is no time!" The man pulled a knife from his belt, a curved blade that was nearly a short sword in length. "Away with you!"

"You are right, there is no time for this," Conan said. With that, he drew his own broadsword and swung it, taking off the hand holding the knife, as well as the head behind it. The big man, no longer so tall, dropped like a sack of wheat.

"Into the boat!" Conan ordered.

Tair, Cheen, and Hok obeyed.

Next to them, with a hiss and a roar, a dock covered in thick pitch flashed into a long sheet of flame.

Conan shoved the boat, putting his legs and back into the move. The boat slid into the water and moved easily away from the land. At the last instant Conan leaped, landing next to Cheen.

Tair already had one of the oars up and in the lock, and Hok was straining to lift the second oar when Conan grabbed it from him and thrust it into place. "Move aside," he commanded, catching the handle of the second oar.

This was not an art at which the Cimmerian was particularly skilled, rowing, but strength counted for a great deal. Conan pulled the wooden blades through the water, using the great power of his arms and shoulders, leaning back into the movement, and the boat sped away from the shore and burning dock at a speed equal to a sluggish runner.

A shed on the dock collapsed, sending a shower of sparks at the boat, but only a few cinders reached them.

As Conan rowed, he looked at the village. It seemed to be a single sheet of flame now, with only a few surviving figures on the edge of the water outlined against the raging inferno.

"The weed is not far," Tair said.

Conan nodded, but did not speak. There was a large enough stretch of water between the village and the weed so that the fire would not reach it, even if the weed was apt to burn, probably unlikely for a water plant in any event. He would worry about the weed and its dangers later; now, he had to escape the edge of the fire.

Conan rowed, and the boat slid across the water to safety.

When Thayla and Blad reached the land's edge, there were only a pair of boats left, and those the object of contention among a group of perhaps fifteen men. The men flailed at each other with fists and feet. A few used knives or sticks, and for good reason. The small boats might each possibly hold four or five passengers safely; more would sink the craft.

Thayla did not hesitate. She ran straight for the nearer of the boats. "Blad—clear a path!"

The young Pili warrior lowered the point of his spear and uttered a war cry as they ran.

The villagers were obviously not expecting an attack by the Pili; Blad's war cry, a hissing, screeching, yodellike scream designed to frighten enemies, seemed to do just that. The men turned to look at the two Pili, freezing where they stood.

Fortunately, only one man was directing in their path. Blad skewered him with the spear and hurled the startled victim aside, releasing the spear and man together. Blad veered to his right a hair and slowed, so that Thayla passed him and leaped into the boat. Blad shoved the boat into the water and jumped in behind her. Fetching up a paddle, he stood in the stern and turned back toward the stunned men. The young Pili screeched again and waved the paddle menacingly.

Several of the men started forward as if to chase the drifting boat. Another group of four or five men ran to the last boat, drawing the attention of the ones chasing the Pili.

Thayla found another paddle and began using it, propelling the boat into deeper water.

At that, all but one of the pursuing men turned back and ran toward the one boat remaining. Before they had covered half a dozen paces, the dock next to the boat collapsed sideways, and buried boat and men under a wall of flaming debris. A hot blast of wind hit Thayla, making her gasp, but she did not stop paddling.

The man who had not run to the boat was now in the water; he was a good swimmer. He was able to move faster than Thayla could paddle the boat, and in a few seconds he was nearly to the craft.

"Wait! Let me in!"

"Blad!" Thayla said sharply.

The young Pili turned to look at his queen, and she nodded meaningfully at the man in the water. Blad nodded.

To the man, he said, "Here, catch the paddle!"

When the man drew close enough to reach the extended paddle, Blad jerked it up and snapped it down again. The edge of the heavy wooden implement smashed the swimming man squarely on top of the head.

The sound was quite loud, Thayla thought as she watched the man sink. A lot of bubbles came up where he went down, but the man did not rise again. Good. They were free of the burning land. Thayla pulled her paddle from the water.

"Take us to the weed there, Blad," she ordered.

She had in mind waiting there until the fire died down, then returning to the dead village and home. Surely her husband or Conan, or both of them, had perished in the fire. Her quest was therefore over.

It had been a near thing, but she felt a lot better now.

Kleg twisted and leaped over a fallen timber that tried to roast him. The dried mud was sloughing off his skin in flat chunks, but it still offered him a fair amount of protection. There was but one more obstacle between him and the water, a low wall of fire fed by a line of tar spilled from a flaming barrel that had tipped onto its side next to where the dock had been.

The running selkie pulled the pouch from his belt and tied it securely around his neck. The pouch bounced on his chest, cracking away more mud, but the weight of the Seed within was the important thing.

Kleg leaped the line of fire, felt it scorch his legs, and came down not on flat ground but on a piece of red-hot iron, some kind of brace from the dock. He was not prepared for the misstep, and his left ankle twisted. He heard a *pop* in his ankle and knew he had done some damage.

His next step told the tale. When he put his left foot to the ground again, he fell. Some ligament had torn and his ankle would not support his weight.

Behind him, the barrel of pitch exploded, slinging globs of fire out in a fountain. One bit of pitch landed on Kleg's right boot. Desperately he pulled the boot off and flung it away as he managed to come up to a one-legged stance on that same foot.

The water was only a few spans away. He hopped.

A river of burning pitch flowed toward the selkie. He glanced backward and saw more barrels of the stuff starting to burn. If they all went up at once, he would be bathed in the boiling tar!

Kleg hopped for all he was worth.

The barrels blew apart behind him, but he was already diving into the cool safety of the lake when the sheet of deadly pitch arced toward him. When the tar splashed into the water, Kleg was half a span deep and still diving.

He began the Change, and in a matter of moments, he had no more worries about what dangers the land might offer. He was long, sleek, and deadly, and aside from a sore fin on his left side, had never felt better in his life.

That which had been manlike bared its teeth in a fearsome grin and swam once again in the waters of its birth.

EIGHTEEN

Conan rowed the small boat to the sloping edge of the weed. When the bow struck the plant, it was as if they had hit solid ground.

The four of them climbed out of the boat onto the mat, and Conan found that indeed the substance seemed very solid. The leaves he saw lay curled tightly against the vinelike runners. Those finger-thick strands of the material, easily visible in the light of the burning village, ran back and forth in a kind of tight weave that supported Conan's weight with a spongy consistency much like damp forest ground covered with leaves and humus. The plant had a distinctly sour, almost fishy odor.

Several boats in the water still moved toward the Sargasso, but none came near where Conan and his friends stood. There might have been other survivors already on the strange weed, but the surface was uneven, rising up into small hillocks here and there, forming shallow trenches in other places, and he did not see anybody else. What an odd thing this Sargasso was.

Conan turned back toward the village, which was now engulfed in its entirety in raging fire. Even where the flame stopped short of the water, the heat must be of killing intensity, to judge from the hot wind that reached him here, hundreds of spans away. If anything still lived within the confines of what had been the village of Karatas, surely it would soon be charred beyond recognition.

As he watched, a great spinning column of fire formed and twisted across the beach, twirling and sending sparks high into the air.

Aye, they had been blessed with good fortune. Many had not been so swift or so lucky.

After a few moments observing the conflagration, Conan turned to Cheen. "It would seem that our quest has ended. If your magical talisman was there"—he pointed at the village—"then surely it is destroyed. I am sorry."

Cheen turned away from the fire, and for an instant Conan mistook her action for grief.

"No," she said. "The Seed is not destroyed."

Conan looked at her, puzzled.

She turned slightly to her right, then her left. She glanced downward. "At least one thief must have escaped. I can feel the presence of the Seed yet," she said, "but it is moving away. There." She pointed at the Sargasso beneath them.

Conan's hand stole quickly to the hilt of his sword, then stopped when its master realized there was no threat. "In the weed?"

"Underneath it. The selkies must still have it. One of them swims away from the fire with it. There."

Conan nodded. This was some kind of magic, Cheen's ability to know such things, and he liked it not. Still, he believed that she spoke the truth.

The Cimmerian turned toward Tair. "Your sister says the Seed survives. If we are to retrieve it still, we shall have to cross this weed after it."

Tair nodded. "Aye. Well, never let it be said that Tair was frightened of a treacherous plantscape and its denizens, not to mention the evil wizard who controls them. I shall follow the thieves to the earth's bowels if need be."

"And I too," the boy added.

Conan looked at the vast expanse of Sargasso, lit here by the flickering orange of the dying village, but invisible farther out into the lake and night. Well. He had come this far; another day or two would hardly matter.

"I am with you," he said.

Tair grinned. "Good. Between the two of us, the Mist Mage's beasts will be as nothing."

Conan could not repress his own grin. He was glad Tair thought so, though his own experiences had taught him to be more cautious in making such statements; still, you could not fault the man's bravery.

"I think perhaps we should wait until daylight before beginning our trek," Conan said.

"Aye," Cheen said. "You are wise."

Conan smiled again. Wise? Hardly. A wise man would likely never have begun this quest. Then again, he had never claimed wisdom. Plenty of time to develop that when his hair turned the color of high mountain snow, his eyes grew dim, and his ears became dulled like an old and rusted blade.

If he lived that long.

The Queen of the Pili and her young trooper left their small boat and began immediately looking for a place to conceal themselves. Blad, as usual, did not comprehend the reasons for their actions, and Thayla was beginning to tire of explaining things to him.

"We are alone, you have lost your spear, and we have nothing to protect ourselves save our knives. Suppose for an instant that you are one of the residents of that torched village yon, huddled here with others of your kind. You did see the other boats?"

"Aye, mistress, but I fail to see—"

"You are no doubt most miserable," she continued over his interruption, "and having lost everything you own, might be feeling more than a little anger along with your sorrow. So you see two unarmed Pili, one of whom is a beautiful female; what might you consider doing to them in your sorrow and rage, were you a man among a group of men?"

She watched as the thought worked its way through Blad's mind. Slowly.

"Ah," he said. "I see."

"Good that you do. Now find us a place of concealment until we can determine who else inhabits this stinking weed."

Blad cautiously led his queen toward a flat-topped hill not far from where they had landed the boat. As they rounded the tangle of growth, they saw a figure crouched in the shadows next to the hill's base. Blad drew his knife.

"Thayla? Is that you?"

The voice was unmistakable, the figure impossible to deny even in the darkness, and Thayla's shock was great and her thoughts near panic. So it was that the Queen of the Pili found her husband, the King of the Pili.

Blad put away his knife. "Milord!"

Thayla ground her teeth as the young fool looked from Rayk back at her, his guilt at having lain with her shining forth from his face like a torch. She had told him that Rayk was most likely dead.

"What are you doing here?" Rayk moved into what starlight the patchy clouds allowed to pass and looked at his wife.

"My lord husband! How happy I am to see you!"

Thayla pushed past the openmouthed Blad and embraced her husband, pressing herself tightly against his body and working her fingers against the muscles of his back.

"Thayla . . . ?"

She dropped her hands lower and pressed his hips toward her own, moving suggestively. "My husband, I thought perhaps you had perished!"

"I very nearly did. But—but—how—why . . . ?"

Thayla's mind worked quickly. She pulled back from her embrace, but kept her hands on her husband's shoulders, gazing lovingly—she hoped it appeared so—into his face. She had to spin a believable tale, and in a hurry.

"A band of Tree Folk attacked our home," she said, glancing peripherally at Blad.

The young Pili stood there, openmouthed still.

"They had with them several barbarian warriors, the like of which I have never known." Well, that was partially true. She had never been with anyone like Conan before.

"We fought them off and pursued them."

"*You* did? Yourself?"

She drew herself upright. "You did not marry a weakling, Rayk."

He nodded. "How true."

"We chased them as far as the Tongue River, and there we saw bodies, fishmen and Pili."

"Yes, yes, we slew them as we crossed the river. Many of our own were lost in the fight."

"I was so concerned that I had to find you," she said. "I feared for your safety, husband."

She watched his face as he assimilated her tale. He nodded, and Thayla breathed a small sigh of relief.

"We have had our own troubles," he said. "A monster attacked us, we lost the fishman with the talisman—I think he still had it—and then the fire . . ."

"Where is the rest of your troop?" she asked.

He shrugged. "Who knows? I found myself alone in a boat at the water's edge, then here. I have seen no more of them. What of your own group?"

"Only Blad here remains." She nodded at the young Pili. "He has been most brave in defending me."

Rayk looked at Blad, who had finally managed to close his mouth. "I shall see him rewarded once we return home."

She was safe! Likely as not, Conan was dead, cooked to a crisp in the blazing village. If he had survived the fire somehow, he was out here somewhere. Once they headed back to the desert, they would never see him again.

"Then as soon as the fire dies down, we can go?"

He frowned at her. "No, of course not. We have not recovered the magical talisman. I am sure the fishmen have taken it to the wizard's castle, in the center of the lake. We must go there and see."

"Are you *mad*? The smoke magician will turn us into jelly! We cannot face that!"

Rayk shook his head, and his face bore that insufferably stubborn look she had grown to hate over the years. "Most of our men have died. We must have the talisman to survive, now more than ever. Do you not recall what you said on the matter?"

"But . . . that was then. It is different now—"

"No," he said, cutting her off. "It is the same. We must find a way to reap some profit from this disastrous venture. Our numbers are too small to survive without help."

Thayla stared at him, aghast. Oh, no! If Conan were out on this weed somewhere, there was still a chance they might meet! And even if they did not, to face the Mist Mage was suicide!

As her mind scrabbled to find a way out of this new danger, Rayk smiled and pulled her against him. "I have missed you greatly," he said. "Come and let us find a comfortable spot to lie down." He handed his spear to Blad. "Stand watch," he ordered. "The queen and I have things to, ah . . . discuss privately."

Thayla felt his hand at the small of her back, urging her away from Blad, who now glared at his king with sudden jealousy and hatred. Rayk did not notice Blad's expression, however, intent as he was on other things.

By all the Gods, were all males so stupid the world over?

Thayla looked over one shoulder at Blad and raised her finger to her lips in a gesture of silence. The young Pili turned away in anger.

How wonderful the world was. One more problem she did not need.

Kleg swam, full of power, through the dark waters, along familiar tunnels through the thick roots of the Sargasso. Light from the moon and stars and even the sun itself never penetrated to this place, but he could see and sense his way quite easily. Uncounted numbers of tiny plants lined the sides of the tunnels, plants glowing with a cold inner fire that produced a pale bluish green light. And even had the plants not done so, a Changed selkie had organs that allowed a kind of vision in almost total darkness. Kleg could not have said how this sense worked, but it gave him an awareness of anything living for nearly the same distance as he could see on land under the stars. The larger the creature, the more aware of it Kleg became.

At the moment Kleg was most glad to have such a sensing mechanism, because he was aware of something following him. Something very large indeed, larger than he in his Changed form was, and not far behind. Fast as he was and traveling at top speed, Kleg could not outswim his pursuer, and that worried him greatly. He had a suspicion as to what the thing was following him. The same beast that he had seen in the village. Whatever its intentions, the selkie was not enthralled with the idea of allowing the thing to catch him.

Kleg knew he could not maintain his current speed for long, that he would tire and have to slow. Whether the thing behind him had to do likewise was another question he did not care to risk his life upon. So—what was he to do? He could continue to swim until exhausted, a thing that would happen long before he reached the safety of the castle. He could turn and fight, and despite his present powerful form, he had few doubts about how that would end. He could try to talk to the monster. Ho, what a choice *that* was!

So, what was to be done?

The glimmering of a fourth idea began to shine inside the selkie's head. His injured foot had been greatly healed by his Change—small wounds were usually cured completely by the process for some reason—and were he to return to his manlike form, the ankle would hardly trouble him at all.

He could not outswim the beast in the water, but perhaps he could outrun it on the weed? Big as the thing was, it would find the going harder on the Sargasso than would a man, surely. There were places where the weed was as treacherous as a swamp, full of danger, but perhaps Kleg could use that to his advantage. Certainly there were more places to hide than in a narrow tunnel. All in all, being on top of the weed seemed at least marginally safer than swimming under it, at least at the moment.

Yes. There were places where the tunnel sent side branches toward the surface. Kleg would find one of them and use it, and perhaps leave his pursuer behind. Mayhap it was not the best thing to do, but it seemed to be the least dangerous option he had at the moment.

The Prime selkie swam onward, searching for his escape.

NINETEEN

Dimma floated about his throne room, angry, but not uncontrollably so. His selkies should have returned by now. They must have met with some difficulties; like as not, that fire on the far shore had something to do with them. He resisted the idea he had formed earlier, to send more of the lake's thralls to search for Kleg and his brethren. The eels and the sirens would keep any intruders from water and weed, and the Kralix would find the Prime selkie, alive or dead. He did not worry over the safety of the sexless monster. It would take a mighty warrior to disable the beast, much less kill it.

So, what was to be done?

Nothing more than he had already initiated. To send forth an army of lake creatures would serve no purpose. Did Kleg survive, he would return, and if he did not live still, the Kralix would find whatever was left and bring it back. Simple enough.

Over the centuries, Dimma had learned patience, though he had done so grudgingly. Once he attained the flesh again permanently, he could indulge himself. Until then the most reasonable course was simply to wait.

Though it was the wisest way, Dimma did not have to like it, however. Best that his Prime selkie have a very good excuse for being tardy when he did arrive. A very good excuse indeed.

Came the dawn, and the fire still burned upon the hapless village, though much diminished in intensity. What remained standing of Karatas was little: a few stone chimneys had survived the heat, but little else.

Conan had arisen with the coming of daylight, and he and his three companions saw clustered on the weed others who had survived the fire's wrath. Knots of men, women, and children gathered here and there, most still watching the burning of what had been their homes.

"Ho, look there!" Tair said, pointing.

Two men came toward them, and Conan's sharp blue eyes recognized them as Tree Folk from Tair's group. Of those who had accompanied Cheen, there seemed to be none left.

Cheen and Tair went to greet the two survivors. Hok moved to where Conan stood. "Are we going to the wizard's castle, Conan?"

"Aye, so we are."

"Will there be danger?"

"Likely."

The boy appeared to consider this for a moment. "Well, probably he does not eat people."

Aye, Conan thought, but his experience with wizards had shown him that those who dabbled in magic could, and often did, do worse than simply eating people. He did not speak this aloud, however. No point in worrying the boy further.

Tair and Cheen returned with the two men of their tribe.

Tair said, "Ah, such tales these tell. They speak of a giant beast who seems part frog, a beautiful lizard woman, and they claim also to have seen one of the selkies. Such boasting!"

Coming from Tair, the accusation of braggadocio was amusing. But Conan fastened upon the sighting of the lizard woman. He asked the men about it.

"Aye, a blue-skinned beauty she was," one of them said. He was short, stubby, and dark-skinned. Conan recalled his name as Stead. The other man, taller and more fair, was named Jube.

Stead continued. "Had another with her, a male, young looking, but full-grown. We would have followed them, but the fire drove us in different directions."

Conan considered this news. The Pili woman was most likely the same one he had met in the caves. It had not been an unpleasant experience overall, but he did not think she was here to thank him for it. No, if Pili women were like those of his own kind, they did not take kindly to being left abruptly without warning or explanation. Like as not, she and her companion had perished in the fire—Conan had seen no signs of any Pili on the weed after their arrival—but a man could never be faulted for vigilance. He would stay alert.

There was a tangled hillock nearby, and Conan took his leave and approached the growth. Climbing it was not much different from climbing a normal hill covered with thick underbrush. Once he attained the top, he stood and looked around.

The vantage point gave Conan clear sight for some distance in the early-dawn light. The castle was a low, sprawling affair rather than one weighted with high towers, and he judged he could walk there in a few hours, had it been over level ground. Given the terrain, however, it was hard to say how long it would require to attain the structure. It might take the better part of a day; much depended upon what dangers might lay hidden in the Sargasso, ready to prey upon an unsuspecting traveler.

In other directions, Conan espied more folk from the destroyed village. He did not see any Pili or selkies, nor did he see any froglike monsters. That was a point in their favor, at least.

The Cimmerian descended from the hillock and returned to his companions.

Stead and Jube had not only managed to outrace the fire, but had looted a vendor's stall on the way, and they thus had in their possession a long row of linked sausages, several oiled-paper packets of jerked beef, and even a few loaves of crusty bread. It was to this meal that the six sat before starting their journey. At least they would travel with full bellies, Conan thought, and that was another point in their favor. A hungry man sometimes made mistakes, and he had the idea that to make a mistake in the wizard's domain might well be fatal.

Conan chewed on a bite of bread and wished he had a cup of good wine to wash it down. He was not afraid of what might lie ahead. After all, he had recently survived a confrontation with Crom Himself—what could be more dangerous than that?

Thayla's breakfast was a raw fish, taken by Blad's spear. Well, actually, it had been Rayk's spear, but it was now wielded by the younger Pili. The flavor of the fish was not unpleasant, though she would have risked a fire to cook it had it been up to her. The king would have none of that, however, and she had to admit he had a point. He was not altogether stupid when it came to matters of strategy and tactics.

When the king moved to a clump of weed nearby to relieve himself, Thayla took the opportunity to speak to Blad.

"What is it?" he asked. His voice was surly.

"Do not act so foolishly, Blad! He is my husband."

"So I heard all through the night."

"It is not him I desire."

"Oh? You gave a good imitation of it!"

"Fool! I had to so that he would not suspect that it is you I want for a husband."

Blad turned to face her, surprise on his features. "Really?"

So young. And so stupid. Aloud, Thayla said. "Of course. He is old and weak. You are young and strong. How could anyone not prefer you to him?"

Blad practically preened as he swelled with pride.

Gods, males were so easy to manipulate. "This is a dangerous undertaking," she continued, "and perhaps the king will not survive it. When we return to our home, I shall choose a new consort." She laid one hand on his shoulder and stroked him briefly. "Whom do you think my new consort will be?"

"Milady, forgive my stupidity—"

"Shh. The king returns. We shall speak more of this later. Only know that I am yours, Blad my stalwart."

As Rayk made his way back from the call of nature, Thayla turned to smile at him. She had both males where she wished them to be. Her sated husband suspected nothing about her and Blad, much less Conan, and if he lived to return with her to the caves, then she would casually mention that Blad had made improper advances toward her during their earlier adventures. Poor Blad would sprout a forest of spears before he could open his foolish mouth.

Then again, did the king meet with some mishap, Thayla would need a companion to protect her until she could reach safety. Blad would do until then.

In any event Blad would eventually have to die. He knew she had lied to her husband about the attack on the caves, and of course, he had a much larger secret in his possession, their illicit coupling. Even with the king dead, Blad would know that the queen had been willing to lie with other than her husband, and he could hardly forget that, even were they to marry. He would always be suspicious that what she had done once she might do again. And rightly so, she knew. So, in any case, Blad could not be allowed to live once Thayla was in a place of safety again. At the moment, however, she preferred to have two devoted males protecting her instead of one.

"We shall depart immediately," Rayk said.

"Of course, my lord," she said.

When the king turned away, Thayla winked at Blad, who smiled and nodded in return.

The thing dogging Kleg had not slackened in

its pursuit, and the selkie was growing tired. He would have to find an exit soon—

Abruptly Kleg's senses detected something ahead of him. It danced at the edges of his perception for a moment before he recognized it for what it was. Or, rather, what *they* were: eels!

Kleg felt a stab of fear. The eels almost always stayed far down in the lake's depths, where they were no danger to anyone save those bottom fish unfortunate to be touched by them.

He had touched one of the eels once while in his water form, and the sensation had not been pleasant. The brief contact had caused his muscles to quiver uncontrollably, and had sent a flutter through him that had been hot and cold, a burning, freezing paralysis. A single eel was not a killing danger to a full-grown selkie, but were his senses correct, there were half a dozen at least in his path, and that many did pose a deadly threat. Once an eel had discharged its power, it was helpless for a time; the one that had touched Kleg long ago had found itself bitten in twain as soon as the selkie had recovered sufficiently to do so. But six at once, that was another matter.

The monster chased him and the eels lay ahead. Had Kleg any doubts about leaving the water for the surface, those doubts were now extinguished like a candle in a windstorm.

The weed above the swimming selkie was thin, though there were no openings apparent in it. He could wait no longer. In a few heartbeats, there would be a tangle of eels, selkie, and monster, and Kleg did not wish to enjoy that particular gathering.

Kleg reached deep within himself and found a bit of fear-inspired strength. Using all the power he possessed, he increased his speed to its utmost. He guided himself to the very bottom of the tunnel, so that his ventral fins skimmed the weed. Then Kleg pointed his nose toward the roof of the tunnel and drove for all his worth straight up.

He hit the roof like a blunt spear, hard.

The thin weed could not withstand the force of Kleg's impact. The driving selkie tore through the material as a needle pierces cloth.

Such was his speed and force that Kleg passed through the weed and more than his own body length into the air. He fell back and flopped onto the Sargasso much like a beached fish.

Quickly, the selkie assumed his man form. He was safe from the eels, at least, and mayhap they would give the monster something to worry over.

The leather sack and strap had survived the impact and still hung safely around his neck. He was naked otherwise, his clothes having been shredded and lost when last he had Changed, but that did not matter. The air was warm above the weed and he needed no protection from the weather. That was the least of his worries.

The Prime selkie trotted away from the hole he had torn in the weed, hurrying in the direction of his master's abode. Perhaps the eels would kill the thing chasing him. Perhaps not, but in either case, he was not waiting to see.

TWENTY

Conan led the five Tree Folk across the matted Sargasso, moving cautiously. There were many places where the uneven surface dipped or rose enough to block the Cimmerian's view for any distance, and he avoided these spots as much as possible. Additionally, he had several times put one foot down on patches of weed that started to give under his weight. Only his quick reflexes saved him from falling through the weed into whatever might be waiting in the water beneath.

They were skirting a wide patch of this thin weed when Cheen stopped and closed her eyes.

"The Seed," she said softly. Then, louder, "It is no longer under the water. It is ahead of us, there!"

She pointed straight ahead.

Before Conan could stop him, Jube lunged forward. "Where? I will retrieve it!"

The man only managed three steps before he sank from sight through the weed. "Aahh!" Water sloshed up through the hole he had made.

Conan moved to the edge of the broken weed and dropped onto his belly to spread his weight. He reached down into the gap. "My arm, take my arm!"

Jube came up sputtering, thrashing at the water, and shot a panicked hand upward. By some good fortune, he managed to clasp his hand around Conan's wrist.

Conan had him now. He began to edge backward from the hole, using his feet and free arm. This was a danger averted—

Suddenly Conan felt sensation grip him, a feeling unlike any he had ever known. It was somewhat like the way his hair sometimes stood on end on a cold and dry day, but that was as close as he could come. His body tingled with a cold fire, his muscles felt as if they belonged to another man, and he convulsed in a spasm that jerked his entire frame, flinging him backward and away from the hole.

Jube's grip was broken, and well that it was so, for the man's fingers had become with the tingling as powerful as a wooden clamp. The sensation stopped when contact ended.

Jube screamed, and his body contorted, his arms shaking. For only an instant his shriek lasted, then he slid back into the hole, and the black water covered him.

Conan was paralyzed; he could not seem to gather his strength to rise. A strange, buzzing sound came from the hole in the weed. After a moment, it stopped.

Cheen and Tair rushed to help Conan to his feet. Brushing them aside, he arose on his own, feeling shaken but otherwise undamaged.

"Crom, what was that?"

He moved back to the hole, carefully, and peered down into it. As he watched, Jube's body floated up to the surface. Tair would have reached for it, but Conan held him back.

"Nay, hold a moment."

"He will drown!"

"Touch him and you may die also. Here, let me have your spear."

Tair tendered his weapon. Gingerly, Conan prodded the body with the wooden butt of the spear. The sensation he had felt was either gone or did not travel through the wood. He pushed the end of the haft under Jube's leather belt, heaved, and managed to lift the man half out of the water. Another tug, and Jube was clear, lying on the weed.

Conan released the spear and reached out to touch Jube with one finger, very carefully. Nothing amiss now. He rolled the body over onto its back.

"He is dead," Cheen said, saying aloud what Conan already knew."

"Aye."

"There is not a mark on him, no wound, nothing. How could this be?"

The man's face was contorted into a grimace that indicated he had died in great pain.

"He looks just like old Kine did after the lightning hit him," Tair said. "Only his face is not black."

"Lightning does not strike underwater," Cheen said.

"Perhaps it does in the wizard's domain," Tair said.

Conan, meanwhile, had edged back to the hole and now peered into the water. Something was moving under the surface. He raised the spear and suddenly jabbed downward. The point struck something, and Conan flipped it up into the air, slinging it free of the spear. For the brief time that the spear had been in contact with the thing, he felt another of those shivery cold fires dance in his hands, but considerably weaker than before.

The thing fell onto the weed, and Conan went to examine it, followed by the others.

"What is it, a snake? Was he bit?" That from the boy.

Conan squatted next to the wriggling creature, being careful to avoid touching it. It was as long as his arm, and the thickness of his wrist. "Not a snake. An eel."

In truth, while the thing looked more like such a beast than anything else, it was not exactly like any eels Conan had seen before. Still, the name was as good as any.

"I have never heard of an eel with poison," Cheen said.

"I have," Conan said. "But I do not think ube was bitten. This thing contains some ower. Kin to the lightning, perhaps. I think hat just touching it is worth your life."

The eel's wiggling slowed and grew less, ntil finally it stopped altogether.

"Well," Conan said, "magic or not, it can be illed. But we had best be certain to avoid alling into the water."

They all turned to look at the unfortunate ube.

Blad led the way, testing the weed with his pear and hesitant steps. Rayk followed, and hayla was behind him.

"Husband, I would not have you think me ritical—"

"Hah!"

"—but," she continued, ignoring his interrup-ion, "what is it you think we are going to do vhen we arrive at yon castle?"

"I shall think of something," Rayk replied.

"That would be a first."

"Hold your tongue!"

"Do you perhaps think that you and Blad nd I are going to storm the place and wrest rom a wizard something he so obviously wants? he three of us?"

"You try my patience!"

"Nay, I merely seek answers. I concede the alue of the Tree Folk's talisman, but trying to eard the lion in his own den seems less than vise."

"I said that I will think of something. W
must first get there and see the lay of the
situation. I shall speak of it no more. And
neither shall you."

He turned away from her, and Thayla stared
at his back. By all the Gods, he was a bigger
fool than even she had thought. He seemed
intent on getting them all killed. Well, that
would not do. More and more, it seemed as if
Blad was a better choice. When the opportunity arose, she would speak to the young Pili.
Convincing him to put a spear into Rayk's back
should be easy enough. Then the two of them
could turn around and go home. With Rayk
dead, things would be a lot easier to manage.
He had gotten more arrogant of late, and a
more tractable mate was definitely in order. A
shame it could not be Blad, since he was
already hers, body and soul, but she could
hardly trust a male who knew too much, which
Blad certainly did.

Ah, well. There was no help for it. If she
wanted to survive, she would simply have to
make some hard choices. One could not have
everything, though one could certainly try.

From ahead, there came an eerie wailing
sound. It was the cry of some creature, and
there was something about it that both at-
tracted and repelled at the same time. Thayla
could not recall ever having heard the like. If
she had been made to describe it, she would
have said the sound seemed to be a lonely

reature who was part wolf, part human woman, nd part swamp loon. It was not so much a owl as a song, and it made her skin crawl.

The three Pili stopped.

"What is that?" Thayla asked.

"How should I know? You have spent as much time on this smelly plant as have I."

"Should we investigate?" Blad said.

Rayk and Thayla spoke together as one:

"No," she said.

"Yes," he said.

"It might be useful to us," the king allowed.

"And it might have us as its next meal," the queen countered.

"I feel drawn to see what makes the sound." t was Rayk who said this, but Blad nodded his agreement.

"Aye, I also feel the attraction," Thayla said, "and that is reason enough to avoid it."

The two Pili males looked at her as if she had prouted wings and might fly away at any moment.

"It sounds like some kind of lure," she said, rying to be patient.

"How can you know this?" Rayk demanded.

"I cannot. But I thought you wanted to go to he mage's castle and retrieve the talisman?"

"Aye, that is true."

"Then you must decide which it will be. Vould you collect the magical device or go hasing off in the weed after some unknown ound that might be deadly?"

She watched Rayk and Blad look at each other. The sound called louder to them than it did to her, that was apparent. Males were prey to drives that did not seem to afflict females, and this soulful song dragged insistently at them.

The king turned to look in the direction of the sound, and Thayla pointed at Blad, catching his attention. She shook her head from side to side, indicating that she did not want to seek the source of the mournful tune calling to them.

Blad, dull as he was, understood. When the king turned back toward Thayla and her lover, she nodded at the younger Pili male.

He found his tongue. "Ah, perhaps the queen is right, Majesty. Our goal is the talisman. We could investigate the sound on our way back."

The king glared at Blad, then at Thayla. He nodded, somewhat reluctantly, the queen thought. "Very well. First we fetch the talisman."

The three turned away from the sound and proceeded toward the unseen castle in the distance.

Thayla's brief moment of triumph and satisfaction faded quickly. Going from one unknown danger to another was hardly a thing to inspire a feeling of victory.

Though better at home in the water, Kleg had spent more than a small portion of his life above it upon the surface of the Sargasso. He knew many of the dangers it held and how to

void them, and he used that knowledge now
s he ran across the living mat. He stayed well
way from the large tangles of vegetation,
specially those with large gaps in the weave.
hose mounds sometimes contained predators,
anging from a ratlike scavenger the size of a
og to cattle-sized crustaceans that could snip
land selkie's arm off with one snap of a
incer.

Too, there were patches of trap weed scat-
ered here and there, though a careful eye
ould detect those from the slight change in
oloration from the normal surface.

Whatever it was that dogged his trail was
ideed slower upon the weed than under it,
nd Kleg steadily gained ground upon the
iing. He would be tired when he arrived at
ie safety of the castle, but if things continued
s they were, he would arrive there well ahead of
is chaser. Kleg managed a smile. This entire
ffair had been more than he had anticipated,
ut at last it was nearing the end.

A distant call reached him, a seductive song
iat flowed over the running selkie like warm
oney.

Kleg's smile increased as he recognized the
ound: skreeches.

Having spent most of his life on and under
ie Sargasso, the Prime selkie knew well the
ire of the skreeches. He, like his fellows, was
ractically immune to the call. Partially this
as due to long exposure, and partially it was

because He Who Creates had designed the skreeches to attract men and not selkies. What might cause one of Kleg's brothers to feel merely a wistful desire would overpower most men. A man would go to a skreech as a bee went to a flower, feeling the attraction until the skreech fastened her teeth in his throat. Those teeth were hollow fangs, the largest of which were the size of Kleg's fingers, pointed like needles. A hungry skreech could drain the blood from her victim in a matter of moments, turning the strongest man into a pale, dead husk to be cast aside. Not a pleasant death, Kleg thought, after having seen a few. There had been a time when men sometimes chose to dare the Sargasso, and any who survived the sight of a companion taken by a skreech certainly never returned.

Once, in the village, Kleg had questioned a survivor of a skreech encounter. It had been most amusing. The man had paled and made warding off signs at the very mention of the things. Mermaids, he called them, though Kleg had not known the term. Like a beautiful woman from the hips up, the man had said, and a fish from there down. That was an apt enough description, Kleg knew. Beautiful, until she opened her mouth and sank those teeth into you.

He darted to one side, to avoid a patch of trap weed.

The skreeches were not his concern. Even if

he should fall prey to one, his strength was more than a man's and equal to the bloodsuckers; besides, it was said that a skreech did not care for the taste of selkie.

Kleg put one hand up on the pouch that still hung around his neck. The talisman was within, and he was nearly where he needed to be. His master would be pleased.

At the moment, Dimma was not in the least pleased. Some unseen crack in wall or floor or ceiling admitted a cold draft of wind, and that small stirring was enough to send the Mist Mage floating down a dank hallway quite against his will. He tried to concentrate hard enough to slow or stop his passage, but it was to no avail.

Dimma raged soundlessly. Five hundred years he had suffered! It was too much! He would, by all the Gods, spend at least the next five hundred years venting his anger upon anyone who crossed his path for the indignity of it all. It was only just that tens of thousands should suffer and die to make amends for his own suffering. Men, beasts, forests, all of them would pay.

The warmth of his anger flowed through the filmy substance of the Mist Mage, giving him the determination to resist the small breeze that wafted him where it would. Dimma floated against the wind, feeling more powerful than he had in ages.

Oh, yes, certainly, he thought, you are strong enough to resist the breath of a mouse, eh?

Wait, he told himself. Wait until I am flesh again! Every mouse for a week's journey in any direction will die!

Along with everything else!

TWENTY-ONE

As the day wore on and the sun rose higher to splash its warmth upon Conan and his four companions, the Cimmerian began to feel more at ease upon the weed. As a matter of course, he avoided any clump or hillock of the plant that might hide an attacker. After observing several more places where the Sargasso was too thin to walk upon, he noticed that such places were lighter in color than the thicker places, a faint, but definite difference. He avoided the lighter patches and the footing stayed firm.

Alas, Conan could not see how they would reach the castle before dark, traveling in such a roundabout manner. To circumvent some of the obstacles took them far to the sides at times, and sometimes the places upon which they could safely walk required a wide detour to find.

As the light of noon shone upon them, they stopped to eat the last of the food Stead and the late Jube had stolen in the village.

"Good that you found this," Conan said, chewing on a greasy sausage.

Stead said, "Yes. Jube did not die with an empty stomach."

He said this as if it were important, and both Tair and Cheen nodded in agreement.

Conan swallowed a bit of the sausage and bit off another chunk. He could not say that dying with a full stomach was better than leaving this world with an empty one. The choice for him was between living and dying. Alive, a man could always find something to fill his belly. Dead? Well, that was another matter, and though it came to all eventually, Conan was in no hurry to try that option as yet.

To amuse himself, Hok dug at the weed with the point of the short knife Tair had given him, and he looked happy in that small chore. Conan smiled at the boy. It took little to keep a child amused.

"What do you think we shall find when we arrive at the castle?" Cheen asked.

Conan shrugged. "Who can say? Your magical Seed, if our luck is good. Perhaps some valuables the wizard is not using. Or maybe a hundred armed selkies instead." He did not worry about such things. He would face it when it arose, and to worry overmuch about it now was merely wasted effort.

Before Tair could speak to that, there came a

haunting sound unlike any Conan had ever heard. His ears were keener than those of his companions, who did not seem to hear it at first. A woman singing some sad and compelling melody, it sounded like.

Tair noticed it; Conan saw him turn his head to better hear the tune. Hok lifted his head from his digging at the weed, Stead caught the sound and finally, Cheen looked around, apparently puzzled.

"What is that?" Tair said. "I have never heard anything so . . . beautiful!"

Aye, Conan agreed. The singing conjured up visions of women lamenting the loss of their men, calling for someone to come and help them forget their sadness. Anyone would do, but they would prefer Conan, as if they could see him there, listening.

Already, Tair was on his feet, as was Hok. Behind them Stead had taken several strides toward the call. Cheen continued to look puzzled.

"What are you doing?" Cheen asked.

Conan ignored her and began to follow Stead. The boy and his older brother had already started in that direction.

"Conan? Tair? Wait!"

Something about the call was familiar to Conan, but he could not say what it was immediately. It was as if he had heard it before somewhere. . . .

It felt like a dream to him, a vision fueled by the sweetness of those voices. Familiar, yes, but

where and when had he heard it before? Surely
he could not forget such women?

Behind him, Cheen yelled. "Conan! Stop!
Something is wrong! Do not go to them!"

She was like a buzzing mosquito, meaning-
less, and Conan continued to walk. Fortunately,
there seemed to be little or none of the thin
weed between him and the women, and—yes,
he could see them in the distance, perched on
the edge of a small lake within the confines of
the Sargasso. It was hard to tell at first, but as
Conan and the others drew closer, he could see
that there were three of them, and they were
all naked as well. Their beauty matched their
songs. They were lush of breast, had long,
black hair that fell to their hips, and—what
was this? Their legs were joined into a single,
greenish body that ended in a tail!

Well, no matter. They were not women, but
certainly they were close enough. And they did
need him so. Their song told him.

Conan grinned. Yes.

He started to move faster.

Something snared Conan's legs, locking his
ankles together. He was unprepared for it, and
he toppled forward. He threw his arms out to
stop his fall and the weed was forgiving, but
his legs were still snarled in something. He
looked back.

Cheen had grabbed him around the ankles,
and she held tightly to them now.

"Let go," he said.

"Conan, no! Something is amiss here!"

"Aye, release my legs; that is what is wrong!"

"No."

No? Well, he would see about that. There was no way she could hold him, he was much too strong. He pulled one leg free, drew his foot back, and was about to thrust his heel into her face—

Then he remembered where he had heard the call before.

In the underground caves where he had been trapped with Elashi the desert woman and the old warrior Tull, there had been some magical, evil plants that had used a voice inside their minds to lure Conan and his friend close. They had very nearly died as a result.

The plants had sounded much like these half women just ahead sounded.

By Crom, it was a trap!

Conan stayed his foot. "I am free of the spell," he said to Cheen. "Release me so that we might save the others!"

"Are you sure?"

"Hurry, woman!"

Cheen let go of Conan's leg, and he bounded up. The song still droned at him, seductive and insistent, but he knew it for what it was now, and the naked women with their arms outstretched toward him held no allure.

The other two men and the boy were still enthralled, however.

To Cheen, Conan said, "Take the boy. I will stop Tair and Stead!"

The Cimmerian began to run.

*   *   *

Thayla had been unable to speak to Blad alone. Her fool of a husband had not moved more than a few spans away from her since the dawn. Did he suspect something? No, she could not see how that was possible, but certainly he had not given her an opportunity to speak to Blad without being able to overhear them, not since he answered nature's call that morning. She had gone off to do the same several times since, trying to offer a suggestion to him to do the same again, but he had not done so. And she could hardly ask Blad to come with her when she squatted behind a clump of weed; fool that he was, even Rayk would look askance at that.

Thayla was beginning to feel desperate. They had to be getting closer to their destination, though they had not sighted it for some time. The way was roundabout, certainly, due to dangers real or imagined, but eventually the three of them would reach the castle, were they not killed by something along the way. To continue onward was to court certain death, Thayla felt, and if she could not get Blad's attention soon, she had in mind using her own knife to slit Rayk's throat.

Better that Blad should do the deed, in case something went wrong, but someone had to do something soon. This was lunacy. Thayla was not ready to die, not for a long, long time.

*   *   *

As the late-afternoon shadows began to paint the hollows and hillocks of the Sargasso, Kleg drew ever nearer the abode of his master. Not long now. He could make out the details of buildings, could see the low and rambling structures that made up the entire compound. He would be there well before darkfall, the hero returned, the instrument of his master's salvation. Surely He Who Creates would be so filled with gratitude that Kleg's reward would be boundless.

Behind the running selkie, the drone of the skreeches lay faintly on the air. Apparently they had yet to ensnare their prey, for when that happened, the songs died more quickly than the victims.

And as for the beast that trailed him, Kleg had neither seen nor heard from it for a long time, hours at least. Whatever it was, whatever it wanted, it would not have from Kleg, for He Who Creates could destroy even such a monster as that one with a few well-chosen words, of that Kleg was certain.

The Prime selkie continued his thoughts of glory and reward as he ran. Soon. He would be there soon.

"Hold!" Conan said as he ran past Tair and turned to face the man.

The tree dweller's face had the look of one who had consumed too much wine. He seemed to be in a trance, staring past Conan as if the

Cimmerian were not there. He did not slow his steady gait toward the singers.

Peripherally, Conan caught sight of Cheen as she grabbed Hok. The boy struggled with his sister, fighting to free himself, but she was bigger and much stronger. Those muscles Conan had admired came into play, and the boy was held fast, despite his efforts to break free.

"Tair, you must stop. This is some kind of trap!"

Still Tair ignored Conan's warning.

The big Cimmerian considered the problem. How to stop the man without injuring him greatly? True, he could catch and hold Tair, but doing so would engage him, leaving Stead to continue toward the singers.

Conan decided what he must do. He clenched his right hand into a fist, and using this knotted hammer of flesh and bone, he punched Tair. He struck the tree dweller high on the torso, just under the breastbone.

Tair's wind left him with a strangled rush, and he dropped, doubled over to his knees, temporarily unable to breathe. As he clutched at his belly with both hands, Conan turned back toward the fishwomen and Stead.

Too late.

Stead was within a span of the nearest woman, and what happened then would stay with Conan forever. The woman smiled, and her lips kept spreading wider and wider, revealing a mouth that was impossibly large and teeth that belonged on a great cat or perhaps a dire wolf. That maw gaped, and the thing that looked half woman and half fish lunged at Stead, clasping him to her breasts and sinking those horrible teeth into his neck.

Stead struggled, the spell broken, but it was beyond him to break free. He screamed. Blood ran from the terrible wound in his neck, spurting and spraying over the monster clamped to him.

Crom! Conan jerked his sword from its sheath and leaped toward the thing killing Stead. So lost was it in its meal that it did not seem to notice Conan.

Blued iron flashed in the light of the setting sun, and the blade whistled as Conan whipped it down as might a man splitting wood with an ax. He had to slash to one side, to avoid striking Stead.

Sharpened iron met the flesh and bone of the thing's right shoulder and cleaved the arm free.

It screamed then, an inhuman screech that hurt Conan's ears. Dropping Stead, the thing moved for Conan like a striking serpent, wiggling on the ground, its remaining arm extended, hand hooked into a sharp-nailed claw.

Conan stood his ground, snapped the sword up over his head, and brought it down with all the strength of his massive shoulders and arms behind the cut.

The blade split the she-creature's head in twain.

The dying thing twisted away in a final spasm and lay quivering on the weed.

The second of the singers slithered over the weed toward Conan. He leaped forward to meet her, and she reared up, balanced impossibly on that tail, arms spread wide to grab him. Conan shoved the point of his blade at her heart and ran her through.

She grabbed the sword in her hands and more blood flowed as her fingers were sliced open on the sharp edge, but such was her strength that she wrested the weapon from Conan's grasp as she fell dying to join her sister on the Sargasso.

Conan twisted to face the third monster as it came for him. He prepared to grapple with the thing as it rose up from the snakelike sliding.

But just as the she-thing reached its full height, it sprouted a spear where its left eye had been.

The creature screeched and fell over backward, both hands wrapped around the haft of the spear that had pierced its brain, killing it.

Conan turned and saw Cheen standing there. Hok lay at her feet, looking dazed. He nodded at the woman. Once again that well-muscled arm had thrown true. She had saved him once more.

Stead, however, was beyond help. The side of his neck was a raw wound that had drained his life's blood. Even had Conan been able to reach him sooner, it was unlikely such a gaping hole could have been successfully stanched.

Conan rose from his examination of the dead

man and retrieved his sword. Cheen, Tair, and Hok approached.

"Is he . . . ?" Tair began.

"Aye," Conan said.

"What *were* those things?" Hok asked.

Conan shook his head. "I know not. I do know that this Sargasso is no place for us. The sooner we are away from here, the better."

"We had better hurry," Cheen said. "We do not wish to be out here after darkness."

Aye, there was a wise comment, Conan felt.

He said, "To the castle, then. We have scores to settle with whoever set these things against us."

"Aye," Tair said. "That we do."

TWENTY-TWO

As the sun gave up his daily reign over the earth and night began to creep out around the edges of the world, the Palace of the Sargasso loomed into Kleg's sight. Close as he was, he could see the pair of selkies standing by the southwestern-most entrance, their tall lances next to them.

At last! He was all the way home!

When the guards saw him, they snapped to alertness, their lances pointed toward him.

Kleg had a moment of worry. Was something wrong?

Then he saw the two recognize him. They relaxed their fighting stances and ordered their weapons.

Kleg released his own tight carriage and slowed to a more comfortable walk.

"Ho, my lord Prime," one of the guards said.

Kleg nodded imperiously. "How stands the watch?"

The other guard, one of Kleg's nest mates and therefore allowed a certain leeway in his speech with the Prime, said, "Dull, brother."

Kleg grinned. While all selkies were brothers, some were more so. The southwest entrance had always been considered an important post because it was nearest the kitchens. A quick guard could dart in and secure a succulent morsel—or one of the kitchen maids—and be back on his post before anyone was the wiser. Kleg knew, for he had once stood this same watch himself.

"See that it stays that way," Kleg said.

He strode past the pair to the first set of tall doors. He worked the latch, pushed the heavy wooden door noiselessly open on well-greased hinges, and stepped inside.

A torch lit the entranceway, showing the next set of doors, only two strides away. Beyond that portal was yet another, smaller door. Each of the forty-six entrances to the palace was constructed in a similar fashion. Even on the windiest of days, a careful passage through the triple-protected entrances would stop even the faintest breeze from coming into the castle. In the form that he wore, He Who Creates could not abide wind, and woe to anyone who forgot that.

Kleg had not gotten to be Prime by being careless. He waited until the air was absolutely still before moving to the second portal, then did the same with the final door.

Inside the palace proper, Kleg moved along the wide torch-lit corridor. He Who Creates would not likely be found here; torches offering a stirring of the air, that also did not please the master.

Not far along the corridor, however, there was a peculiar beast sleeping upon a tattered rug. This creature, another of the master's creations, appeared to be kin to wolf and ape, having the body of the former and the head of the latter. He Who Creates had named these things vunds. It was not very intelligent, the vund, but it was fast on its feet and it could repeat simple messages entrusted to it.

Kleg kicked the vund. It jerked awake with a start and stared at him.

"Go and find the master of the palace and say to Him, 'Your Prime has returned.' Do you understand this?

The vund blinked.

"Say it."

The thing's voice was near a growl, but understandable enough: "Yur Prime 'as return'd."

"Good. Go. Hurry."

The vund loped off down the corridor, half again as fast as a selkie could run. Wherever He Who Creates might be in the castle, the vund would find Him. The palace was huge, but the vund would search until it located the master of it and everything else within the walls.

Kleg himself headed toward the special room in which certain magical devices had been placed. Once He Who Creates got the message he had sent, it was a certainty that that was where Kleg would find him.

The torches on the walls burned steadily, disturbed only by the wind of his passage as Kleg went to meet his master.

Simple-minded as it was, The Kralix held steadfastly to its one goal. It had been given a task, and its entire being was focused on that chore. Find the One. Bring the One. Allow nothing to stand in your way.

It was hungry but it did not pause to eat. The One was still ahead of it somewhere; the Kralix could feel the One as it could feel the weed under its feet and the air on its skin, and it had to get to the One and bring it.

Dimly the Kralix realized that its position was such that it would not have far to go once it caught the One. The One was going in the right direction on its own, and that was good, but the Kralix had not been instructed about that. It had been told three things only: find the One. Bring the One. Allow nothing to stand in your way.

Tirelessly, the Kralix lumbered on, fulfilling its mission.

Night had cast its net of stars into the sky when Conan and his party arrived next to the castle on the Sargasso.

To their left and a hundred spans distant, a pair of guttering torches lit a wide double door set in the flat wall between the torches. The flickering lights also showed two selkies standing guard.

Hidden by the cloak of night, Conan and the three Tree Folk were invisible to the selkies, but even so, the Cimmerian motioned for the others to crouch low, and when he spoke, his voice was nearly a whisper.

"We have arrived," he said.

"Aye," Tair said. "Now what?"

Conan considered. A direct attack was possible, the odds being three to two in their favor, but he did not know but that the guards could call for quick help. Having a score of fishmen pour forth from the door might well be possible, and he did not like those odds.

They could perhaps work some sort of trick on the guards. Conan could draw their attention to one side, say, while Tair and Cheen circled around behind. Could they lure the fishmen away from the door, that would keep them from seeking help.

Or perhaps they could steal close enough in the darkness to spit the pair with two well-thrown spears. Cheen was certainly adept with hers, and Conan had no reason to believe that Tair was any less skilled.

But as he pondered these things, the burden of choice was lifted from them.

A monster stalked out of the night and charged the two selkies.

Tair saw it first. "By the Green Goddess, look at that!"

Conan did not need to be told again.

The thing was easily twice the size of an ox, wide-legged, and its smooth, mottled skin glistened under the torches. It looked to be some kind of water beast, Conan thought, but with claws and fangs like that of a bear of mayhap a direwolf. It thumped heavily across the weed directly at the door.

The two selkies leaped forth and attacked, jabbing with their lances, but they were as wasps stinging a man. One of the selkies ventured too close, and those massive jaws crunched him with a sound loud in the night. Conan shook his head. A quick death, at least.

The second selkie hurled his lance and the long point of it sank deeply into the monster. The creature spat out the first selkie, and paused long enough to pluck the lance from its side with one forepaw, flicking the weapon away as might a man brushing dust from his cloak. Then it lunged, fast for so large a beast, and used the same paw to claw at the second selkie. The fishman was opened from chest to groin by the swipe, and fell backward, mortally wounded.

The monster paid the dead and dying selkies no more mind, but turned toward the door and hurled itself at the portal. The stout wood cracked and splintered under the impact. The thing opened that hideous mouth and attacked the shattered door with those pointed fangs, chewing through the wood.

"It eats the door," Hok said incredulously.

Indeed it was so, Conan saw. The three of them watched in astonishment as the monster devoured enough of the door to gain passage. Once it moved from sight, save for the hindmost part of it, there came another crash as something inside fell prey to the thing's teeth.

"Must be an inner door," Conan said.

After a few moments, the monster disappeared completely, not without more sounds of destruction.

The night grew very quiet after that.

Tair and Cheen and Hok looked at Conan, wonder in their faces.

"I do not know what it is," he said, in answer to their unasked questions, "but it has provided us with an entrance. If you are still interested in going inside to find your Seed?"

Thayla's fear was high in her now, and not without reason. There had been no opportunity to speak alone with Blad, and her husband seemed preternaturally alert, so that using her obsidian blade on him had been impossible.

Now he had led the trio to the castle itself, and they moved parallel to the long wall, searching for an entrance.

"Hold!" Rayk whispered hoarsely, waving at her and Blad to get down.

Thayla obeyed and, in a moment, saw the cause of her husband's caution.

Oh, no! It was Conan, and some of the Tree Folk!

The big man led two adults and a child across a short stretch of open weed toward the castle. Following their path with her gaze, Thayla saw what lay ahead of the four, and it was an amazing and grisly sight.

Two of the fishmen lay sprawled on the weed, mangled corpses both. The remains of a shattered door hung on the wall, lit by a single torch that hung loosely above and to one side of it.

"What—?" Thayla began.

"The beast in the village," Rayk answered before she could finish her question. "I have seen its work before."

"What is it doing *here?*"

Rayk shook his head. "I know not, nor do I care. It has given us a way inside, we should be thankful to it."

"What if it waits within?" Blad asked.

"What of it? It will dine on those four before we attempt to enter."

Thayla watched Conan steal across the ground, his sword lifted and ready. "And if it is still hungry when we get there?"

"Then we shall wait until it leaves."

"Rayk, I think this has gone far enough."

He turned to face her. "I am king, Thayla, and it matters not what you think."

She stared at him as he turned back to watch the four men cautiously enter the castle through the shattered doorway. Truly he had lost his reason. She reached for the knife at her belt. Best to stab him now and flee.

But Rayk was up and moving toward the castle. Thayla glanced at Blad.

"Come along!" Rayk ordered.

Before she could speak, Blad stood and followed.

Fools! All males were fools! They would get her killed yet!

"Thayla!"

Reluctantly the Queen of the Pili stood and hurried after her husband. She had no wish to remain alone and unprotected out here. Besides, Conan still lived, and if the thing that had torn its way into the castle had moved on, the big man would likely continue to live. If he and Rayk chanced to speak before she could prevent it, things would become very tricky and dangerous indeed. Best she be next to Rayk to prevent such a thing from happening.

Silently, the three Pili followed the four humans into the wizard's domain.

Dimma hung quietly in his sleeping chamber, trying to close his mind and rest. The chamber had been designated for sleeping because it was the stillest in all the palace. Surrounded on all sides by other rooms and with the doors closed, it was as dark as new pitch and unstirred by even the faintest wind. Like a cave in the bowels of the earth, the silence here was almost a tangible thing.

Sleep was not forthcoming for Dimma, however; his mind darted birdlike from perch to perch, too agitated for rest.

Came a knock at the door.

Despite his unrest, Dimma did not allow himself to be disturbed while in this chamber, not for any reason. Whoever did so courted a quick and messy death, and Dimma willed himself toward the floor so that he might better see the fool he was about to slay.

"Who dares?" he called out.

"M-m-my l-lord?"

It was the voice of his sub-Prime selkie.

"Enter and meet your doom!"

The door opened, very slowly, so as not to stir the air in the room, and the selkie stood there. One of the vunds sat near his feet.

"Have you a final word before you die?"

"M-m-my lord, the v-vund, it h-has a m-m-message."

"Then it shall die as well." Dimma raised one foggy arm and prepared to cast a spell of burning at the two. He could do that much on his own, at least.

"S-speak!" the selkie said to the vund.

The vund stood and took a deep breath. Its last, Dimma thought and he cocked his hand to throw the spell.

"Yur Prime 'as return'd."

Dimma held his hand. "What?"

The vund repeated the message.

Such joy shot through Dimma that he instantly dropped his hand, the burning spell forgotten. Could it be true? After all the centuries?

"What is this beast's station?"

"The s-southwest d-d-door, my lord."

Dimma laughed. It was some distance away, that entrance, but even so, his Prime would be halfway to the strong room by now. "Away with you!" he ordered. "To the strong room!"

The sub-Prime and the vund hurried away, and Dimma willed himself after them. The end of his torment was near!

Moving as fast as he could, the Mist Mage floated through his palace toward his redemption.

TWENTY-THREE

When Kleg arrived at the strong room where all but one of the elements of a particular magic spell were stored, he was met by the master of the realm, the Abet Blasa, Dimma the Mist Mage.

He Who Creates floated half a span from the floor.

"My Prime. Do you have that which I dispatched you to fetch?"

Still naked save for the pouch around his neck, Kleg nodded. He fished the Seed from the bag. "Aye, my lord."

Kleg felt the wizard's joy almost as a tangible thing, a blast of heat from an open hearth. Then, "What took you so long?"

Kleg began to explain. "The journey was fraught with deadly peril, my lord. Pili and monsters and—"

"Never mind, never mind, it matters not. What is important is that you have the talisman. Quickly, place it in the niche!"

The selkie hurried to obey. Within the strong room, guarded ever by four of his brothers, Kleg saw the other elements of the spell set in their places. Here stood the skull of a long-extinct big cat; there in a wooden case was the cloak of a witch; over there, a wax-stoppered bottle filled with a black liquid that had once been the blood of a minor demon. There were more than a dozen such exhibits, and the only one lacking was the Seed that Kleg even now placed with great care into a sconce set near one wall.

"Everyone out," He Who Creates ordered.

Kleg scurried to obey, along with the two guards who had been with him.

"Close the door."

One of the guards pulled the door shut, carefully, so as not to stir the air, and looked at Kleg. "What happens now, Prime?"

"He Who Creates will work a spell," Kleg replied. "And in so doing, he will create a new self."

Kleg turned back toward the closed door. His master had not exactly been effusive in his praise. On the other hand, Kleg still lived, and considering how long it had taken him to accomplish his task, that was not something at which to sneer. After the spell was done, perhaps He Who Creates would be feeling more generous. Kleg intended to wait right here and find out.

The Prime selkie's intention was thwarted, however, when he heard heavy footfalls approaching down one of the long corridors and caught a fetid odor he recognized immediately.

The monster! It still pursued him!

Kleg's thoughts jumbled upon themselves. How could this be? If that thing could follow him here, into his master's domain, what did it mean? What could he do?

Full of sudden fear, the Prime selkie started to knock at the closed door, to ask He Who Creates for help—then he stopped. To disturb his master now would likely be worth death. Better he should lead the thing away. He could outrun it easily enough, he knew that, and if the beast outrun it easily enough, he knew that, and if the beast caused He Who Creates distress while He was performing His spell, that would likely bring swift death as well.

Kleg said, "A thing will pass here in a moment, seeking me. Stay out of its way. Allow no one else to disturb our master!"

With that, Kleg turned and ran off down the corridor.

Dimma's pleasure was unbounded. The ingredients he had spent most of his lifetime collecting were all finally assembled. The spell itself required nothing more now save that he pronounce it aloud, something he could do easily even in his present form. There were

three short verses to the incantation. He had
spoken them in practice so many times they
were as familiar to him as his own name.

The Mist Mage drifted over the floor to the
center of the strong room. He took a deep
breath and began to intone the words of the
spell that would make him whole at last.

No one had challenged Conan and the three
Tree Folk as they moved through the long
corridors. They had seen no more guards, nor
anyone, for that matter. Conan found it odd.

"Certainly is still," Tair said. "The place feels
dead."

Indeed, the air was motionless. The torches
on the walls burned steadily, sending their
smoke straight up to paint dark the high
ceiling with nearly perfectly round pools of
soot.

"I do not like it in here," Hok announced.

With that Conan agreed, though he did not
voice it aloud. Instead he said, "Cheen?"

She pointed down the left branch of a corridor that forked just ahead of them. "The Seed
is that way."

The four of them made the turning.

Conan's plan for retrieving the talisman was
somewhat vague, but direct in intent at least.
They would find a way to steal it, were it
unguarded, and if it was protected, they would
slay the guards, take the magical Seed, and
flee. He preferred simple plans, and this one
seemed basic enough. If possible, they would

void the wizard. If he could not be avoided,
hen they would slay him and then depart.
Simple.

Thayla allowed her husband to move away
rom her, slowing her pace so that she dropped
back far enough to whisper to Blad without
being heard. She had to keep her voice very
ow indeed, so quiet was the corridor.

"Milady?"

"The king is mad," she said. "He will cause
he death of us all."

"But what is to be done? He is the king."

"Not if he is dead." She reached out and
ouched the shaft of Blad's spear meaningfully.

"Milady!"

"Hear me, Blad my stalwart. If he dies, then
ou will become king and my consort."

The young Pili's eyes widened. If he had any
spark of ambition at all, this ought to fan it
nto a flame.

"Thayla! Blad! Why are you tarrying?"

The king had stopped and was looking back
t them.

Thayla stopped and bent. "A stone in my
oot, Rayk." To Blad she said, "Hold still, that
may lean against you." She pulled her boot
rom her foot and made as if to empty the
nonexistent stone from it onto the flagstone
loor. As she leaned against Blad, she allowed
er hand to stroke a sensitive area of his body,
nseen by the king.

Blad gasped at her touch.

"What is it?" the king asked.

"Uh ... uh ..." Blad said, obviously at a loss.

"The point of my dagger has accidentally pricked him," Thayla said hurriedly.

"Well, put your boot back on, withdraw your blade, and let us continue."

Rayk turned away from them, and Thayla gave Blad a hot look. The youth had the spear. She hoped he would use it, and soon.

Kleg knew the corridors of the palace as well as anyone, and he dodged through them now, leading the thing behind him on another chase. Had it been sent by some rival wizard? What was it? Would He Who Creates bother to deal with it, once He had finished His spell?

Too many questions and not enough answers.

As Kleg ran, he took care to double back on his trail every so often so as not to get too far away from the strong room in which his master worked His spell. He had not eaten or rested for what seemed a long time, and he was tiring. Best he be close when his master finished His current chore so that He Who Creates could take care of this thing chasing him.

Conan sensed someone around the corridor's next turning, and he waved his companions to a halt as he went to see who—or what—it might be.

The Cimmerian crouched low and slowly moved to peer around the edge of the wall. A

uick glimpse was all he needed. Just around
he corner stood four selkies, each armed with
  spear, bracketing a wooden door inset into
he wall.

He moved back behind his cover. Whispering
uietly, Conan said to the others, "I think we
ave found your Seed. There are selkies ahead,
uarding a door."

"Yes, I can feel the nearness of the Seed,"
heen said.

"Very well. There are four of them and three
f us," Conan said.

"Nay, there are four of us!" Hok allowed. He
ounded indignant.

"Very well, four, then. If we attack quickly,
ve can overcome them and retrieve the stolen
eed."

Tair hefted his spear. "Aye. I am ready."

Cheen nodded.

Conan drew his sword and took a deep
reath. "On my count of three," he said. "One.
wo. *Three!*"

With that, the Cimmerian leaped around the
orner and sprinted toward the guards.

"Shhh," Rayk said, waving for Thayla and
lad to halt. "The Tree Folk and that large man
re just ahead."

The three Pili crouched, and Thayla moved
nough so that she could see that what Rayk
aid was true. The four humans were likewise
rouched at the juncture of two corridors not
ar ahead of them.

"They do not know we are here," Rayk said. "We can steal up and slay them before they notice us." He drew his obsidian knife. "Ready your spear," he whispered to Blad. "You take the big one, I will cut down the female and the smaller man. Thayla, you kill the child."

"Rayk—" she began.

"Silence! Do as I order!"

Moving with great stealth, the three Pili crept up behind the four. Thayla risked a glance at Blad, who returned her look. She nodded at the king, then at Blad's spear. Now is the time, she thought.

Just as Rayk gathered himself to leap, Thayla heard Conan begin counting. What was he doing?

When the big man reached the number "three," the entire group leaped up and darted around the corner.

The move caught the Pili by surprise.

After a moment, Rayk said, "After them!"

With that, the king jumped up and ran around the corner.

Blad and Thayla followed.

Two verses of the spell were complete, and Dimma had just begun the third when he heard some kind of commotion in the corridor outside the strong-room door.

The Mist Mage frowned. His concentration was broken, and he mispronounced the third word in the second line.

"Set and Drakkar take you!" he screamed

Now he would have to begin the spell again! Oh, whoever had caused this was going to die! But not now. Everything could wait until he was finished.

He began the first verse of the spell again.

In his near exhaustion, Kleg had allowed the monster to gain upon him. It dogged him closely now, only a dozen spans behind, loping along in a slow, but steady run that never seemed to vary, shaking the walls as it moved.

Ahead was the corridor that led back to the strong room. Kleg was nearing the end of his strength, and were he to survive, he would have to do something soon. Perhaps He Who Creates was finished with the spell by now. Even if his master was not, Kleg felt as if he had no choice. He had to have help with this thing, and soon. If nothing else, the guards might be able to fight it to a standstill.

Calling upon the last of his reserves, Kleg increased his speed a final time and rounded the corner.

As the selkies turned to face the unexpected attack by Conan and the Tree Folk, the Cimmerian looked past them to see another selkie dash round the far corner toward them.

A moment later, the monster who had chewed its way into the castle also came round the turning.

Conan slashed at the startled guard and his

blade bit deeply into the selkie's skull, dropping him.

"Conan!" Cheen yelled. "Behind us!"

Conan spun past the other guards and, in turning, saw a trio of Pili armed with knives and a spear, charging toward him, weapons raised to strike.

Crom! What was happening?

Selkies, Pili, Tree Folk, and a giant monster all ran pell-mell toward each other. The corridor was chaos. Confusion reigned.

So much for a simple plan.

TWENTY-FOUR

Kleg rounded the corner nearest the strong room and faced more than he had expected. What was this? Men and Pili, battling with his brother selkies!

Unarmed and naked, Kleg would have turned back, but the monster behind him forbade that option. Given no other choice, he ran forward to join the fray.

Thayla ran next to Blad. "Now!" she commanded. "Kill him now!"

Blad glanced at her. Confusion lit his face. "Which one?"

"The king, fool! Use your spear!"

Conan parried the second guard's lance point and cut at the selkie's belly. The wounded guard doubled over and dropped his weapon.

The Cimmerian spun away, slinging blood from his blade as he cocked it over one shoulder against the next enemy foolish enough to get within range.

To Conan's left, Tair traded jabs with the third selkie guarding the door, while Cheen and Hok worried the fourth guard with spear and knife.

To his right, the Cimmerian saw three Pili running closer. The leader held only a knife, but the one behind him carried a spear. The third Pili was the female with whom Conan had been intimate, and she was screaming something he could not quite understand.

The Pili would get to him in a moment, so Conan shifted his stance to await the charge.

But as the leader of the lizard men approached, he suddenly threw up his hands and screamed. The knife flew, bounced from one wall, and clattered onto the flagstones.

Conan was puzzled, but only for a moment. As the leader fell, the one behind him jerked the spear from the dying lizard man's back and raised the weapon in triumph.

"I am king!" he yelled. "Long live the new king!"

Conan leaped forward and thrust his broadsword into the Pili's chest.

The Pili blinked and gave Conan a look of absolute surprise, then pitched backward and fell flat upon his back, his open eyes still staring.

A short reign to be sure, Conan thought.

"May the Great Dragon shrivel your manhood!" the female Pili screamed. She drew her knife and leaped at Conan.

He hated to cut down a female, but if the choice was her life or his, Conan was prepared to decide it in his own favor.

He did not get the chance, however. Something slammed into his back and sent the Cimmerian sprawling. On the way down, he lost his sword.

Thayla's rage wrapped her like a cloak as she lunged toward Conan, her knife set to gut him. But the selkie who had come running around the corner ran smack into the barbarian and the two tumbled to the floor. Thayla leaped to one side and barely avoided being knocked over by the tumbling pair.

She moved back toward them, knife lifted. If the selkie bested the man, then she would sink her blade into his back. If Conan survived, she would do for him likewise.

The man was strong, Kleg thought as they wrestled on the floor, maybe twice as strong as any the selkie had ever faced, but he was thrice as powerful as a man, and this contest would be his.

Not easily, though. The man shifted, and his muscles bulged as he avoided Kleg's hands on his throat. The pair rolled, slammed into a wall, and it was Kleg who took the brunt of the impact. The selkie's grip was broken and

the man took advantage of this to slip free. The
man dived, rolled, and came up, fists doubled
to strike.

Kleg came to his feet and observed the man.
He obviously intended to box, and even a
weaker opponent could defeat a stronger one,
did his blows land solidly. Kleg shifted warily
to his left—

The selkie's foot touched something cold on
the floor and he spared it a fast look to see
what it was.

The man's sword lay there.

Quickly as he could, Kleg squatted and
snatched up the weapon. The man was too far
away to get to him before he completed the
action.

Kleg grinned as he hefted the weapon. "Prepare to die," he said. He stepped forward,
raising the sword easily as he moved, and
made to slice the man in twain.

"Look out behind you, fool!" a female voice
called.

Kleg ignored the cry. He was not stupid
enough to fall for that old trick.

Then he caught the stink of his nemesis and
felt the hot breath of the thing on his back. No!
He tried to turn, but it was now too late.
Everything went dark.

The last thing the Prime selkie felt was the
sharp teeth of the monster closing on him.

Thayla screamed a warning, but the fishman
paid her no mind. The monster behind him

opened hellish jaws and bit the selkie, taking his whole upper body into its mouth. The thing lifted its victim from the floor and shook it like a dog shakes a rat. Bones crunched. Blood oozed from the selkie.

The Queen of the Pili stared in horror, but the monster had no apparent interest in her or anyone but the selkie. The beast turned away, the surely-dead fishman securely in its mouth, and padded down the hall toward the door.

Conan also turned to watch the monster, and Thayla realized this was her chance. Of course, the king was dead, but her hatred of Conan had grown enough so that it no longer mattered. She leaped at his back, her knife raised to stab.

"Conan!" a woman screamed.

The man in front of her reacted instantly. He dropped flat, and Thayla's lunge, overbalanced as she was, carried her past. She tripped and fell. She threw both her hands out to stay the fall, but she was too close to the wall. The knife in her hand hit the wall and she could not release it as she continued her headlong fall. She saw the point coming at her right eye and she managed a final scream before the knife claimed her.

Dimma's anger bordered on madness, so black was it. Once again he had lost the words of the spell, such was the uproar outside his chamber.

Before the wizard could restart the first chant, the door burst open, sending a blast of air that battered the Mist Mage and knocked him across the room almost to the ceiling.

"Who *dares*!"

When Dimma had righted himself, he saw the Ranafrosch standing in the shattered doorway, the body of a selkie clenched in its jaws.

"Not *now*, you moronic beast!"

The Ranafrosch dropped the body onto the floor. It thudded against the flagstones and lay still. The monster looked at Dimma like a fetch-dog at its master.

Dimma's rage exploded and he cursed the thing, extending one wavering hand that sent a beam of heat and light splashing over the beast like a bucket of fire.

The Ranafrosch's skin blackened and crackled under the magical attack. It emitted a moan and fell, rolling over onto its back. The stink of its flesh filled the air.

Dimma managed to will himself back into position over the various talismans and other ingredients.

Once again, he thought. For the last time.

Conan looked at the Pili female. She was dead, sure enough, with that wicked-looking black blade buried in her eye up to the hilt. Killed by her own hand.

He picked up his sword and turned toward his companions. Cheen and Hok had been joined by Tair, and they finished off the last selkie guard as he watched.

The monster, meanwhile, shoved the door

open and stepped inside the chamber beyond. After a moment, the thing was rewarded for this action by a blast of light and a fierce heat Conan could feel even where he stood. All the Cimmerian could see was the thing's hindquarters, but it was apparent that the monster would walk the land of the living no more. Smoke rose from its carcass.

Conan moved to where the three Tree Folk stood.

"The Seed is in there," Cheen said.

"Aye. You see what the monster got for going through that door?" Conan said.

"We have come too far to realize defeat now," Tair said. He started for the door.

Conan sighed. Aye, that they had. He made after the smaller man, and Cheen and Hok followed.

The Mist Mage was nearly done with his spell. A few words more and he would regain the flesh permanently. He felt a surge of happiness build within him, but he kept it from spilling forth, at least until he could say the last line of the spell. Eight words more, six, four—

"There it is!" a woman yelled.

Dimma mispronounced the second to last word of the spell that would have made him whole.

He screamed. "Is there no end to this!"

He turned his attention to the four people who had invaded his chamber. A woman was moving toward one of his talismans. Who were these interlopers? What were they doing here, voiding his attempts to free himself of his curse? ·

The largest man, a barbaric-looking fellow replete with thick muscles, leaped toward Dimma, wielding a sword. The man swung the blade in a manner that would have cleaved the wizard in half, had he been other than mist. As it was, the sword passed harmlessly through him, trailing no more than wisps of fog.

The swordsman looked puzzled, and tried a second cut, to the same end. Dimma would have laughed, had he not been so enraged.

The blast of magical force Dimma had directed at the unfortunate Ranafrosch had almost completely depleted his personal powers; otherwise he would have swept the four from his sight with the same kind of infernal rays. As it was, his ire so disrupted his thoughts that he could only come up with a simple holding spell. He spoke aloud three words and made the proper signs and the four people froze into immobility, the big one with the sword raised for a third strike. The fool would die in that pose, as soon as Dimma was finished with his important business.

To assure his privacy, Dimma floated to the shattered door and peered into the hall. There were a number of bodies lying about, but no sign of anyone else alive to disturb his conjuration. Thank all the base Gods for that!

Dimma returned to his strong room and

began his spell for what he hoped would be the
final time.

Conan felt as though he were bound in an
invisible net; he was unable to move more than
a hair before he met the unseen resistance. He
strained his powerful muscles to their utmost,
to no avail. The wizard had laid some kind of
spell upon them, and whatever he was saying
at the moment, Conan felt certain that it would
not serve him and his companions were the
wizard to finish it.

The mage floated with his back to them, and
Conan could see the wall beyond through the
body of the wizard as the man—was he a
man?—droned out some doubtlessly evil incan-
ation.

But . . . what could he do? He was trapped.
And even if free, he had seen that his weapon
was useless against the magician.

The breath of doom cooled his spine.

Dimma unwound the final words carefully,
all his concentration upon them. Nothing would
interrupt him this time, not if the entire castle
were to sink, nothing!

The last syllable of the last word rolled forth
from Dimma's lips into the still air and hung
there echoing softly.

The wizard held his breath, waiting. He had
done it. Would it work? Would anything happen?

The air about the Mist Mage began to swirl,

he could feel himself stirring. *Some*thing was happening!

The currents of magic within which Dimma had lived almost his entire life also stirred as did the air, drawing into themselves all the esoteric forces available in the room.

It *was* working!

The spell, it seemed, was gathering its own power, pulling energies from the air and water and building to add to its tapestry. It took from Dimma part of his own force; he felt it drain from him, but that meant nothing, for when it worked he would be a man again, and able to command much greater powers than he had as a halfling!

As he felt himself begin to form bones and organs and muscles and start sinking slowly toward the floor, Dimma leaned back his head and howled in triumph. Yes! Yes! It was happening, after all the centuries! At last!

Conan had been trying unceasingly to break the invisible bonds upon him when he felt them suddenly weaken. His upraised arms came down a little, and now the spell felt more like thick mud around his limbs than a tightly wrapped net. He could move, but slowly.

In front of the Cimmerian the magician was growing more opaque and solid, settling toward the floor like a broad leaf falling from a tree, floating gently from side to side.

Conan felt certain that were the wizard to reach the ground and turn, it would be all over

or him and his companions. The spell over his
body weakened a little more, but he was still
sluggish. He would not be able to move fast
enough to chop the mage down; it would be
like trying to move the sword underwater.

As the wizard lowered toward the floor,
Conan also lowered his blade so that it pointed
straight ahead. He could not cut, but mayhap
he could use the point like a spear. He managed a step. His legs felt as if they were bound
in pants of iron, his feet shod in boots of lead.
Sweat broke from his skin as he strained to
take another step. The wizard was only three
spans away, another four or five steps and he
would be there.

If he had the time.

Yes, he was becoming as he once was, Dimma
felt, and in another moment he would be free,
forever. He had already decided how he would
destroy this entire realm. Far below the waters
of the lake, a magical shield kept the molten
rock under it from bursting forth as once it had
ten million years past. He had placed the
shield there when the mountain had rumbled
two centuries ago, linking the protective device
to his own soul. Should he die, the shield
would vanish, and a river of lava would jet up
to boil the waters of the lake before spilling
over the sides of the mountain to cook everything it touched. He could also release the spell
as he transported himself magically away, and
by all the Dark Gods, he would do so!

His feet were nearly touching the floor now, and he knew that when they did, he would have defeated the old wizard's dying curse. He began to laugh. Triumphant, finally!

Conan took another step, the sword held in front of him with both hands. His speed increased a little, but it was still no more than a crawl. Three paces more and he would be there; two ... but—the magician had settled to the floor now, and he was starting to turn—

Dimma felt his muscles tense as they took up his new weight, the floor solidly under his feet. Done. And now to destroy personally those who had dared to interrupt his labors before leaving the molten rock to finish everyone else.

He turned slowly. "Time to die," he said.

With all his strength, Conan lunged. It was slow, the move, but his entire being was behind the sword. The wizard turned as the point of the blade arrived. The broadsword sank into the magician's new body just under the breastbone and continued on, slowly, but surely. Blued iron passed through the mage's heart and between two segments of spine before piercing the skin of his back and then his cloak, to emerge into the still air.

The spell holding Conan vanished of a moment, and the release sent the Cimmerian forward like a hurled rock. His sword's hilt slammed into the dying wizard's abdomen and the mage was knocked from his feet and two spans backward by the force of it. He twisted as he fell, and landed on his side.

"N-n-n-o-o-o-o-ooooo!" was all that he said, a lamenting wail. He shuddered once, and was still.

Dimma the Mist Mage was no more.

TWENTY-FIVE

"Is he dead?" Cheen asked, coming to stand next to Conan.

Before he could speak, the body on the floor began to change. As they watched, the solid form of the Mist Mage began to shrivel, as a piece of fat tossed into a hot fire shrinks. The magician's skin thinned and wrinkled and became like old parchment, then disappeared completely. The flesh under it did much the same, and after a moment only the bones remained, yellowish at first, then turning pale, chalky white before crumbling to powder. The entire transformation took less than a minute, and at the end, nothing remained of the Mist Mage save a thin layer of dust on the flagstones.

"Aye," Conan said, "I would say he is dead."

"Older than he looked, too, I would wager," Tair added.

Cheen turned away and went to the cause of their quest. She lifted the Seed gently from where it lay and held it up before her face, staring at it reverently.

"We can go now," she said.

Conan looked around. "Aye. But perhaps we might tarry long enough to collect a few baubles." His keen eyes detected the yellow gleam of gold in some of the fittings in the room, and surely that faceted green jewel next to the destroyed door was of some value? This venture might prove most rewarding after all.

The floor rumbled beneath Conan's feet, rocking him.

"What was that?" Hok said.

The adults looked at each other. "It felt like an earth tremor," Conan said.

"On the water? Not likely?"

The castle shook again, hard enough so that Conan had trouble maintaining his stance. Cheen fell to one knee, and even the fine balances of Tair and Hok were disturbed. A large crack appeared in the ceiling and dust showered down from the gap.

"Whatever the cause, best we get out of here before it collapses on us," Conan said.

The others followed his lead as the Cimmerian ran for the doorway. He skirted the dead monster, reached out to snatch the jewel from the stand next to the opening, and stuffed the gem into his belt pouch as he ran.

A creature with the body of a dog and the

face of a monkey ran past, looking fearful, and Conan fell in behind it.

"What are you doing?" Cheen asked. "We came in from the opposite direction!"

"This beast lives here, likely it knows the halls better than we."

The dog-thing scrabbled across the stones as it rounded a corner, Conan and the others right behind it. Ahead, a pair of selkies also ran, and if they noticed the people behind them, they gave no sign of it.

The floor shook again, the hardest tremor yet, and even Conan could not stay on his feet. He tumbled, managed to roll on one shoulder and come up without injury. A chunk of the wooden archway supporting the ceiling just ahead of him shook itself loose and fell to the floor with a loud clatter. More cracks laced up the walls and across the ceiling.

Whatever it was that had the wizard's castle in its grasp, it did not appear that the structure would survive.

"Quickly!" Conan ordered.

The other three managed to clamber to their feet to rejoin Conan once again.

The dog-thing was nearly out of sight, but Conan spied it up ahead and once again gave chase.

Through the corridors they ran, with the building shaking and twisting around them, walls starting to collapse, the floor buckling.

Finally the dog-thing led them to a door. It moaned at the closed portal, scratching at the wood with its paws, until Conan arrived. "Move aside!"

The dog-thing obeyed, and Conan twisted the handle and shoved the door wide. Beyond lay another door. They all ran toward it, opened it, and saw yet a third portal. Conan swore and leaped at the final barrier, flinging it wide.

Night still held sway outside, but the stars shined down on them, and Conan led his companions and the dog-thing out into the clean air. A heartbeat later, the Sargasso shook violently and the portal through which they had only just passed collapsed behind them.

"A near thing," Tair said, staring at the fallen doorway.

"We are not safe yet," Cheen said. "Look!"

Conan turned to follow her pointing finger.

In the distance, great clouds of steam rose from the lake, nearly blotting out the moon. The clouds were lit from below by an orange glow.

The weed undulated again, and a roaring sound in the distance came as more steam boiled upward and the orange glow increased in brightness.

"A volcano," Tair said. "The mountain is coming to life underneath the lake!"

Conan nodded. He knew of such things, where the rock itself flowed like honey down the slopes of hollow mountains, burning everything in its path. The lake would boil like a pot on a cookfire, and everything in it would be scalded to death, the weed included.

The Sargasso rippled, and they were all thrown down by the hard wave.

"We have got to get away from here!" Tair said.

Not far from where they lay, the weed tore suddenly asunder, and water splashed up through the rent.

Conan stood. "It is a day's walk to the water's edge," he said.

The Sargasso erupted to his left, spraying torn weed high into the air, and the stench of rotten eggs filled the air. Before Conan could speak, another patch of weed, fifty spans away in the opposite direction, flew upward, and a gout of flame filled the air over the torn weed, roaring and then vanishing as quickly as it had appeared.

"Crom!"

"We will never make it to the shore," Tair said. "Not through *that*!"

"We have no choice," Conan said. "Better to die trying than not."

"Wait," Cheen said. "Maybe there is another way."

"I am open to suggestion," Conan said.

The weed shook again. In the distance, balls of gaseous fire flared and vanished, lighting up the night. A low rumble began and grew louder, and the weed rocked as if it were a boat in a stormy sea.

"The Seed," she said. "It has great powers."

"Enough to calm this?"

She pulled the talisman from her belt and

ooked at Conan. "Nay. But perhaps it can ransport us home."

"What?"

"There is a legend that says one who is attuned to the Seed can call upon it for a return to the grove."

"A legend? Do you know how to invoke it?"

"I am not certain."

A blast of fire rose upward a hundred spans from them, a ball that floated upward into the darkness. The heat singed the hair on Conan's arm.

"Our time runs short," he said. "Try your spell."

"Gather close," Cheen said. "Link hands."

Conan and Tair clasped wrists to the Cimmerian's left, and he reached for Hok with his right. The boy darted away.

"Hok!" Conan called.

The boy ran to the dog-thing and gathered it up into his arms. The thing quivered, but made no resistance as the boy held it, then ran back to where Conan stood.

"What are you doing?"

"It is afraid. We cannot leave it here to die," Hok said.

He hoisted the thing over one small shoulder and grabbed Conan's right hand with his left, then extended his right arm and hooked it around his sister's arm. Tair also linked elbows with Cheen on her right, leaving her hands free to cup the Seed. She started speaking quietly and quickly, saying something Conan could not understand.

The noise of an explosion filled the air. In the distance a fountain of red orange reached from the lake toward the stars. A moment later, the weed began to buck wildly. When the others would have fallen, Conan held them up, using all the strength of his thickly thewed legs to stand fast on the gyrating weed.

Cheen continued to speak in a low, hurried voice.

The weed snapped upward suddenly, like a man popping a whip, and Conan and the others were hurled skyward. Even as they flew, still connected, he glanced down and saw the weed burst open beneath where they had stood, and a ball of fire coming up from the water. Conan sucked in what he thought would surely be his last breath—

When he exhaled, releasing his breath, Conan found himself standing on solid ground beneath the great branches of a giant tree.

"It worked!" Tair yelled, releasing his grip on Conan to clasp his sister to his chest.

To Conan's other side, the boy Hok danced in a circle, clutching the dog-thing tightly. The animal yipped excitedly.

Conan grinned. Magic was by and large something he avoided when he could, but this time he had no problems with this particular example of it. He could not recall looking death

o closely in the eye before. He was most glad
o be alive.

For a moment, Conan thought he heard a
amiliar laugh in the distance. Is that you,
Crom? Making up for your joke by sparing me?
f so, you have my thanks.

The laugh, if there was one, faded, and
Conan's grin grew into a full smile. Tomorrow
e would resume his interrupted journey to
Shadizar. He would bid farewell to Cheen and
'air and Hok and their giant trees, and he
vould go. The wicked City of Thieves awaited
im, its treasures ripe and ready to plunder.

PLAY HYBORIAN WAR

IMPERIAL CONQUEST IN THE AGE OF

CONAN®

BE A PART OF THE LEGEND

Hyborian War, is an epic play-by-mail game which brings to life the Age of Conan the Barbarian. Rule a mighty Hyborian Kingdom with its own unique armies, leaders, and culture — authentically recreated from the Conan series. Cimmeria, Aquilonia, Stygia, Zamora ... choose your favorite kingdom from over thirty available for play.

Play-by-mail with other rulers across the nation.

Every two weeks, your game turn will be resolved at our game center. After each turn we will mail you a detailed written account of your kingdom's fortunes in the battle, intrigue, diplomacy, and adventure which is HYBORIAN WAR.

Be a part of the Conan legend! Forge by your decisions the tumult and glory of the Hyborian Age. Your game turns will be simple to fill out, yet will cover a fantastic range of actions. Send forth your lords and generals to lead the host. Now turn the tide of war with the arcane magics of thy Wizards. Dispatch your spies and heroes to steal fabled treasures, kidnap a mighty noble, or assassinate a bitter foe! Rule and Conquer! The jeweled thrones of the earth await thy sandaled tread.

FIND OUT MORE WITH NO OBLIGATION. WRITE US FOR FREE RULES AND INFORMATION. REALITY SIMULATIONS, INC. P.O. BOX 22400, TEMPE, AZ 85285, (602) 967-7979.

Turn fees are $5, $7 or $9/turn depending on the initial size of the kingdom you choose. The game is balanced with individual victory conditions. So, no matter what size kingdom you start with you have an equal chance of winning. Slower turnaround games available for overseas players.

ASK US ABOUT OUR DUEL-MASTERS™ GAME ALSO!